THE
SHADOWLANDS

EMILY RODDA

SCHOLASTIC INC.

New York Toronto London Auckland Sydney
Mexico City New Delhi Hong Kong Buenos Aires

ISBN 0-439-81707-2

12 11 10 9 8 7 6 5 4 3 2   7 8 9 10 11/0

Printed in the U.S.A.
First American continuity edition, April 2006

Contents

1 - The Forbidden Way

The narrow channel through the rock disappeared into thick darkness, echoing with the hollow sound of lapping water. A broad band of bright pink and yellow seaweed floated across its entrance.

Lief had no need to consult the little map in his hand to know that this grim tunnel was the Forbidden Way — the only path to the island of Keras, and the third part of the Pirran Pipe. But still he looked down at the map and the arrow drawn by the Piper of Auron.

The map had been soaked, marked, and damaged, but against all odds it had survived. Like us, Lief thought, looking up at Jasmine and Barda.

They were both sitting very still, staring at the dark crack in the rock. They no longer had to squint against stinging spray. The Auron guards who were towing the boat had ordered their great eels to slow.

Because Auron boats were narrow, with no room for two to sit side by side, Barda was alone on the central seat, holding the boat's single paddle. Jasmine was at the front of the boat with Kree, whose injured wing was still weak, perched on her shoulder and Filli chattering beneath her collar. Lief was in the back.

"Once we are in that tunnel, there will be no turning back," Barda muttered. "We will have to stay alert."

Lief nodded. Certainly, Doran the Dragonlover, the first explorer of Deltora's underworld, had passed through the Forbidden Way. But that had been hundreds of years ago. Many things might have changed since then.

As the boat's prow nudged the first strands of bright weed, the Auron guards released their hold and moved away. Only Penn, the Auron history-keeper, stayed close beside the boat, speaking softly to the giant eel on whose neck she was perched.

The guards were wild and fearsome, with their clothes of animal skin and wicked bone spears. But they would not cross that bright weed barrier, the ancient Auron warning of danger, unless ordered to do so by their leader, the Piper. And no such order had been given.

"We will give you a boat and guide you to the edge of our territory, but we can help you no farther," the Piper had told Lief, Barda, and Jasmine as they ate their final meal in Penn's little hut. "No Auron may enter the Forbidden Way."

"It is our most ancient law," added Penn, anxious to soften the Piper's bluntness. "Should Aurons enter their sea, the Kerons would attack."

"The Plume people said the same of you," Jasmine remarked lightly. "They said you would kill us on sight."

"The Plumes are lying savages!" snapped the Piper, his eyes sparks of pale fire in his wrinkled face.

Lief and Barda glanced ruefully at each other. They knew that there was no point in defending the Plumes. The old hatred between the Pirran tribes was too strong to be shaken by the arguments of three strangers.

But Jasmine was looking at the two fighting spiders, sleeping peacefully together in their new, large cage. United by fear of a common enemy, Flash and Fury had put aside their bitter rivalry and now wrestled only in play. As a result, they were to stay with Penn, who had grown quite fond of them despite their fearsome looks.

"Even Flash and Fury have decided they have

more in common than they thought," Jasmine said. "But the Plumes, Aurons, and Kerons cling to their bitterness. It is hard to believe that once you were all Pirrans."

"That was long ago," muttered the Piper. "Pirra is the Shadowlands now, and the Plumes and Kerons are to blame. If they had accepted the lady Auron as Piper, the Pirran Pipe would never have been divided, and the Shadow Lord would not have been able to take our land."

Penn's brow creased. She, at least, was clear-sighted enough to admit to herself that the followers of Auron had been just as stubborn as the followers of Auron's rivals, Plume and Keras. The three groups had shared equally in the rash decision to divide the Pirran Pipe.

Now, as the boat rocked gently in the swell caused by the coiling of the great eels, Lief looked up at Penn's anxious face.

The history-keeper had insisted on accompanying them as far as the Forbidden Way, carrying the fire that would light their torches. She had been cheerful on the journey through the rainbow sea, but now her fears showed clearly in her eyes.

Holding her flare high, she urged her eel to the front of the boat and lit Jasmine's torch. Then, silently, she moved back to Lief.

"Farewell, Penn," Lief said. "Thank you for all you have done for us."

"I have done nothing," Penn answered, dipping the flare till it touched the torch Lief held up to her. "But what you have done for *us* can never be repaid. I pray that you — "She bowed her head, unable to continue.

"Never fear," said Barda heartily. "We will live to share Molisk patties with you again, Penn."

"I hope it will be so," Penn whispered. "May Auron protect you."

She murmured to her eel, which obediently moved behind the boat and nudged it forward. The boat slipped over the band of weed and into the mouth of the tunnel.

At once, Lief's mind filled with the sweet, piercing music of the Pirran Pipe. The sound was so loud, so overwhelming, that it seemed to him that Barda and Jasmine must surely be able to hear it, too. But he could see by their faces that they could not.

He stared, transfixed, into the darkness ahead. His mouth was dry, his head ringing with sound. Dimly he realized that he was clutching the cloth bag that hung around his neck, under his shirt. There the mouthpiece and stem of the Pipe lay hidden.

The last piece of the Pipe was calling to them out of the darkness. Calling . . .

Stop this! You must be alert, be ready . . .

Lief forced his hand over the side of the boat, scooped up some water, and dashed it into his face. He gasped as the icy liquid splashed on his hot skin.

The spell was broken. The music faded away, leaving a strange, sad emptiness behind it. Lief blinked rapidly as his eyes cleared.

The light was dimming rapidly. The walls of the passage were racing by. Lief twisted in his seat to look behind him, and was startled to see that the passage entrance was already just a narrow slit of light in the distance.

"What is happening?" Jasmine exclaimed. "Why are we going so fast?"

"Some sort of current is pulling us along," Barda called uneasily. "I am hardly paddling at all, and yet . . . "

"It is the Pipe," Lief managed to say. "I — feel it."

In moments the boat was skimming along in darkness, the passage walls lit only by the flickering yellow light of the torches.

The walls flashed with rainbow colors, which soon gave way to purest green. But above, where the torchlight did not reach, there was only thick black.

Suddenly Kree squawked as Jasmine jerked in her seat and slapped at her neck. "Something just fell on me," Jasmine exclaimed.

"A moth, no doubt," said Barda, concentrating on steering the boat as it raced along. "I have seen a few of them around."

Then he slapped at his own neck. Something had fallen onto the skin there, and was clinging.

Lief felt a tickling on his hand. He looked down and saw a winged, slug-like creature squirming there. He shook his hand, but the creature did not fall away. With a start, he realized that it was biting him — burrowing its head into his flesh.

And it was growing. Its body was swelling as he watched. Filling with his blood.

"Leeches!" he shouted, shaking his hand again, filled with disgust.

He saw Kree fluttering from Jasmine's shoulder as she scrabbled at the collar of her jacket, trying to pull off two leeches that were hanging from her neck. He saw with horror that more of the loathsome creatures had already landed on her hands.

"Beware! Above!" shouted Barda.

Lief looked, and his stomach heaved. The air high above them was teeming with flying leeches, streaming in thick, whirring clouds down from the darkness.

Wildly he waved the torch above his head. Dozens of slimy, winged bodies sizzled in the flames. But still many of the leeches swerved around the fiery barrier to settle on his hands and arms, to feed and swell.

And these were only the forerunners. Thousands upon thousands were following, spiralling downward.

"Jasmine, Barda! Get down!" Lief shouted. Recklessly he cast his torch into the water, then tore off his cloak and threw it across the boat to make a canopy.

In moments the companions were lying face down beneath the cloak, holding it awkwardly in place. A pattering sound began as the first cloud of leeches rained down on their shelter, sensing the warm bodies beneath it. The pattering increased, became a relentless pounding. The cloak began to sag.

Lief's arms and hands were trembling with the effort of holding the cloak in place. The leeches that had been clinging to him before he took shelter, and the few that had found a way to creep under the cloak since then, were hanging like bloated sausages from his wrists and the backs of his hands. He gritted his teeth, forcing down the wild, urgent need to pluck them off.

The loaded cloak began pulling away from the boat's edge. Panic-stricken, Lief heaved at the fabric, trying to tug it back into place. But already leeches were pouring through the tiny gap, fastening onto his hands, slithering into his sleeve.

The cloak bulged and slipped again. The gap at the side of the boat opened further. Leeches poured through in a whirring mass.

We are finished, Lief thought suddenly. After all we have been through, we are lost — defeated by the smallest creatures we have ever faced.

It would have been almost funny, if it had not been so vile.

Even as his hands struggled hopelessly to close

the gap, his mind flew to Del. He would never return. Marilen's worst fears had come to pass.

Yet I regret nothing, Lief thought. I did what I had to do.

A strange peace flowed through him. And with that peace came the music of the Pirran Pipe, piercing him with its exquisite sweetness.

At last, Lief surrendered himself to it. He let himself drift in the tides of sound. His eyes closed.

And so it was that he did not notice that emerald light was suddenly shining through the fabric above his head. He did not notice that the drumming, pounding sound had ceased. He did not hear the soft splash of water as the boat skimmed lightly across a rippling green sea, drawn safely and surely to land.

2 - Keras

When Lief came to himself, the voice of the Pipe had faded and a great weight was pressing down on him. He pushed violently, and at last struggled into dazzling emerald light. Then Barda and Jasmine stirred beside him. As they sat up, the boat tilted under the shifting weight of millions of dead leeches.

The boat was rocking gently in shallow, pale green water that lapped on a sandy shore. Beyond the shore was a forest of fungus trees in soft greens and browns.

"We are on Keras!" Barda said slowly. "We must have reached the end of the Forbidden Way. We came out into the light, and all the leeches died."

Suddenly shuddering, he scrambled out of the loaded boat, Jasmine and Lief close behind him. They plunged their arms and faces into the shining green water over and over again, as if to wash even the memory of the leeches away.

When they felt clean again, they waded to shore, heaving the boat after them. They pulled the craft onto the gently sloping sand and upturned it, emptying it of its vile cargo. Then Lief reclaimed his cloak and they moved on, into the green shade of the forest.

A sandy path wound through the trees. They began to follow it. Now and then there was the sound of a creature scuttling in the sand, but there was no other sign of life. The silence was eerie.

"So, we are in the territory of the emerald," Barda said, in a casual but very loud voice. "Above us is Dread Mountain, where our friends the Dread Gnomes live."

Lief realized that Barda was telling any unseen watchers to be wary of attacking them. Barda sensed, as he did, that the forest was not as deserted as it seemed.

They reached a clearing closely hemmed in by trees. Here the silence seemed thicker. The back of Lief's neck prickled. He looked rapidly around, but nothing stirred.

Jasmine's eyes flicked down to the great gems that studded the belt at Lief's waist. The ruby and the emerald were undimmed.

"The gems cannot be relied upon to give warning down here," Barda muttered.

"So you have told me," said Jasmine. "But why

is it so? The gems first came from deep within Deltora. Surely they should be *more* powerful here, not less."

"Who are you? Why are you here?"

The companions jumped back, drawing their weapons. The whispering voices seemed to have come from all around them. But the clearing was empty.

"Answer!"

Jasmine drew a sharp breath and nudged Lief. Following her eyes, he looked up. A fiery sword hung above his head, point down. Two more swords hung over Jasmine and Barda. Sweat broke out on Lief's brow. Clearly, the questions had to be answered, quickly and carefully.

"I am Lief, king of Deltora, the land above," he said clearly. "My companions are Jasmine and Barda. Many of our people are enslaved in the Shadowlands, and only the magic of the Pirran Pipe will save them. The Plumes and the Aurons have each lent us their part of the Pipe. We have come to beg the people of Keras to do the same."

There was a moment of great stillness. Then, abruptly, the swords vanished and a large group of people appeared out of thin air.

Like the Plumes and the Aurons, the people were small, with pale eyes, long noses, and large, pointed ears. Their garments were shimmering green, and a few, strangely, had yellow hair on their heads.

One of these, a woman wearing a Piper's tall

headdress, moved towards the visitors. Green moths with glittering wings fluttered about the headdress like a moving crown. A boy with a bony, eager face and a mass of spiky fair hair crowded close behind her.

"Greetings, cousins!" the woman said in a low, musical voice that held a hint of amusement. "I am Tirral, Piper of Keras. Please lay down your weapons."

As Lief hesitated, there was a soft, rushing sound. The next moment his sword, Barda's sword, and Jasmine's dagger were all lying at Tirral's feet.

Jasmine and Barda lunged forward, but Lief flung out an arm to hold them back. He had seen what they had not. At the moment they moved, the green moths fluttering around Tirral's head had changed to shimmering arrows, pointed at their hearts.

Tirral, who had remained utterly motionless, smiled.

"Forgive our caution, cousins," she said. "You claim that the parts of the Pirran Pipe you carry were given to you, but it is far more likely that you took them by force."

"It may be more likely, but it is not true," said Lief, slowly dropping his arm. "Keep our weapons, however, if it makes you feel safer."

Barda and Jasmine, their eyes on the hovering arrows, stepped back reluctantly.

The arrows shrank and changed back into

moths. "Thank you," said Tirral calmly. "It would have troubled us to injure kinsfolk. Especially kinsfolk who have done what is proper, and brought with them a fine gift."

"Gift?" growled Barda suspiciously.

"Such a great quantity of bait, heaped on the shore!" the eager-faced boy cried. "Ah, thanks to you we will have fresh-caught Seawing for weeks to come!" He smacked his lips. "Seawing are delicious! And there is nothing they like better than leeches from the entrance to the Keras sea. If only we could — "

"Gathering the leeches is a dangerous task, and we do it rarely," Tirral explained, cutting him short.

"If we lit the tunnel — for just a few moments — " the boy began.

"We cannot light the tunnel, Emlis," said Tirral wearily, as if they had had this argument many times before. "The darkness and the leeches are our protection from the Aurons. Are we to risk daring our enemies to attack us for the sake of a little bait?"

"I am surprised that you need bait for fishing, Piper, since your magic is so powerful," said Jasmine pertly.

Tirral smiled. "There are many ways to catch a fish," she said. "And if the fish you want rises to a simple bait, so much the better. Please follow me."

She turned on her heel and moved away, ushering Emlis firmly before her.

"I hope that *we* are not the fish in this case," muttered Barda as he, Lief, and Jasmine followed, with the other Kerons close behind. "Are we guests, or prisoners?"

"It is not far to go, cousins!" called Emlis, craning to look at them over his shoulder.

"Why do they call us cousins?" said Jasmine, rather too loudly. "We are no kin of theirs!"

"But you are!" said Tirral, stopping where the path ended in a dense clump of trees. "Do you not recall your history?" She turned to face them, and touched the wisps of fair hair that showed beneath her head-covering.

"The Girl with the Golden Hair!" Jasmine exclaimed, astounded. "Alyss and Rosnan! You mean . . .?"

"Certainly," said Tirral. "After they settled on Keras, Alyss and Rosnan had many children. Those children grew up to marry Kerons, and have children of their own. And so it went on through the generations."

"Most of us have some above-worlder blood running in our veins," Emlis broke in. "Even those who do not bear the sign of the golden hair as I do." He ran his fingers through his wiry hair with obvious pride.

Tirral sighed. "And so we greet you as distant cousins, as our ancestors greeted Doran the Dragonlover, long ago," she said. "Doran was not surprised. It was the tale of Alyss and Rosnan which had brought him to the caverns in the first place."

"We were led here by the same story," Lief murmured.

"And of *course* Alyss and Rosnan stopped on Keras!" cried Jasmine. "The emerald cavern is the last before the grey place where they feared to go."

"But who would have thought that after so long there would still be a trace of them here?" Barda exclaimed.

Tirral shrugged. "Blood is blood, no matter how thinly it is spread over the ages," she said. She raised her hand. The trees blocking the path vanished to reveal a large group of startled, guilty-looking children.

"Bad little fish! Did we not tell you to remain hidden in the fruit store?" scolded Tirral. "What if we had been a band of savage Aurons, come to eat you alive?"

She sounded very fierce, but hid a smile as the children scattered.

Now the companions could see that the clump of trees had concealed a village. Without speaking, Tirral led the way through the broad, tidy streets.

The village was large, light, and pleasant. The houses were made of green fungus wood, thatched with dried seaweed. Fish swam lazily in ponds in almost every garden, and the children who had been shooed from the village entrance peeped from behind the garden walls.

At last they reached a large open space, in the center of which a fire burned brightly in a deep cradle of stones. Woven mats were spread on the ground around the fire.

"This is our meeting place," Tirral said, sitting down on one of the mats and signaling for Lief, Barda, and Jasmine to join her. "Here Alyss and Rosnan told their story to our ancestors."

"Doran sat here, too, in his time," put in Emlis, throwing himself clumsily down beside her. "It was Doran who brought the fire that burns here still."

The other Kerons who had been gathering by the fire were all whispering and watching the visitors with interest. But none was as eager as Emlis. Quivering with excitement, he gazed at the visitors, drinking in every detail of their appearance. "That is the Belt of Deltora, is it not?" he breathed, leaning closer to Lief. "Doran said much of its power."

Tirral glanced at him with affectionate irritation. "This is my son, Emlis," she said. "He has more above-worlder blood than most of us, I think, for he longs to travel, and knows Doran's tales by heart. Your arrival has pleased him greatly."

The young man blushed and he ducked his head, muttering awkwardly.

"Now!" Tirral raised her voice slightly. "You are

our kinsfolk and, according to Keron beliefs, it is our duty to help you if we can. Our part of the Pirran Pipe is precious to us, but we can well survive without it if we must. Our own magic is sufficient for our needs."

The people around the fire murmured solemn agreement. Lief's heart began to pound with excitement.

Then, with a stab of dismay, he saw Tirral's face hardening.

Whatever she says of Keron beliefs, she does not want to give up her treasure, he thought. She has found a way to refuse us. A way her people will accept.

"The Pipe will not be lost," he said quickly. "It will be returned to the caverns, I swear it!"

Tirral went on as if he had not spoken. "But also according to our beliefs," she said, "if you borrow something from us, swearing to return it, I may demand something of you to keep as a token of your oath. A thing that is as close to your hearts as our treasure is to ours."

She smiled broadly, showing all her white, pointed teeth.

3 - Song of the Pipe

Lief, Barda, and Jasmine looked around at the silent people by the fire. All were nodding seriously. Clearly, Tirral was speaking the truth.

But it is a trick, Lief thought. She is going to ask for something she is sure we will not give. Glancing at his companions, he saw that Jasmine's hand had crept to her shoulder, where Filli and Kree huddled silently. Barda was frowning, thinking, no doubt, of the sword that had been his faithful companion for most of his life.

Lief thought of his own most precious possessions — the sword forged for him by his father, and the concealing cloak woven by his mother's hands. How could he survive in the Shadowlands without them?

He waited in hideous suspense as Tirral turned to him, her eyes glittering. At last she spoke. "I ask for

. . . that pretty jewelled belt you wear, King of Deltora," she said.

"Mother!" cried Emlis, aghast.

A great, dizzying wave of heat swept over Lief. He heard Jasmine and Barda crying out in amazed anger and the watching people exclaiming, but he felt only sick — sick with relief. He hung his head, knowing that he must not let Tirral see his eyes.

Finally he allowed himself to look up. "Very well," he said. Ignoring Barda and Jasmine's startled protests, he unclasped the gleaming belt and handed it to Tirral.

The watching people gasped in awe. Many jumped to their feet and rushed to crowd around their leader, eager to see the famous belt more closely.

But Tirral's face was a study in baffled rage. Never for a moment had she thought Lief would agree to her demand. Like all Kerons, she had grown up with Doran's tales. She knew how vital the Belt of Deltora was to the safety of the world above.

"Lief, what are you thinking of?" Jasmine whispered furiously.

"Three things," Lief whispered back. "First, we will be in the Shadowlands very soon. Second, the gems in the Belt of Deltora cannot be taken beyond Deltora's borders — a fact that Tirral clearly does not know. And third, this is the safest place I can think of to hide something of great value."

Jasmine's expression changed abruptly. She had

been living in the present for so long that she had actually forgotten that if Lief was to go into the Shadowlands he would have to leave the Belt of Deltora behind.

But Barda's face was like thunder. "Lief," he muttered. "Are you saying that you actually intend to cross the border with us?"

"Of course!" Lief stared at him, astonished. "Have I not always said so?"

Barda shook his head furiously. "Whatever you said, I was sure that when the time came you would come to your senses. Are you mad, Lief? You cannot go into the Shadowlands! You and the Belt are the only things that stand between Deltora and the Shadow Lord. Have you no sense of duty?"

Duty? Lief's fists clenched.

What had his life been over the past months, but a rigid devotion to duty? Had he not worked till his eyes were burning, hidden himself away from everything and everyone he loved? Had he not kept secrets, suffered being criticized, misunderstood — even hated — because the safety of the kingdom was his first responsibility, and enemies were everywhere?

Passionate words trembled on his lips. He longed to unburden his heart at last.

No! You must not weaken now. Especially now . . .

Lief clenched his teeth, fought the hasty words back. "The Pirran Pipe first called to me when I did not even know of its existence, Barda," he said. "I know that I was intended to find it, and carry it on this quest. I will not abandon it now."

"Then I wish we had never seen it!" snarled Barda.

Jasmine was looking worried and uncertain. "Truly, the risk is very great, Lief," she murmured. "Perhaps . . ."

"Jasmine, do not join Barda against me!" Lief cried. "I cannot act against my nature!" Or my heart, he thought miserably. Jasmine, do you not see? Pirran Pipe or no Pirran Pipe, how could I let you go, and not follow?

He became aware that the people clustered around Tirral were drawing back. Tirral was weighing the belt in her hands, bitter contempt mingling with the anger on her face.

"This is not a fair exchange!" she exclaimed loudly. "The belt is all but powerless!"

"Mother, that cannot be!" Emlis burst out, blushing with shame for her. "Doran told us! The Belt of Deltora is as powerful as the Pirran Pipe!"

"In the world above, perhaps," snapped Tirral. "Here, it is just a jewelled trifle."

But the crowd murmured restlessly and, as Tirral looked around, biting her lips, Lief breathed a sigh of relief. Much as she might want to, the Piper could not go back on her bargain now without seeming dishonorable and losing her people's trust.

Stiffly, as though every movement was paining

her, Tirral took from the folds of her robe a small shell box. At the same moment, Lief lifted the red cloth bag containing the mouthpiece and stem of the Pirran Pipe from beneath his shirt.

Tirral opened the box and held it out. The end-piece of the Pirran Pipe lay inside, nestled on a bed of silk. It was very small. Its strange, carved surface gleamed faintly green in the emerald light.

She looked up at Lief and their eyes locked as the music of the Pipe flowed around them.

The people fell silent. They, too, could hear the music. But Jasmine and Barda fidgeted, glancing at one another, for they could hear nothing at all.

Dazed by the music, Lief drew the partly completed Pipe from its covering. Then Tirral handed the endpiece to him, and he fitted it into place.

The music stopped abruptly, as though shut off by a tap.

"It has ceased to mourn," whispered Tirral, and suddenly glistening tears sprang into her pale, cold eyes.

Stunned by the sudden silence, Lief stared at the magical object in his hands. It was shining with a subtle radiance, as though lit from within. Here, at last, was the Pirran Pipe — whole and perfect for the first time since the warring tribes of Pirra divided it and stilled its voice. And complete, it was transformed.

"But, it has changed!" Jasmine breathed in awe.

"It glows! And surely it is bigger than it should be."

It was true. The endpiece of the Pipe had been the smallest part of all, and should have added very little. But now, complete, the Pipe seemed far larger and stronger, far more strange, more beautiful, more thrilling than it had before. It was as though it was greater than the sum of its parts.

But it was silent. Waiting. Waiting for warm breath to bring it fully to life. Waiting for the skilled and loving touch that would call its music back from the ghostly realms in which it had grieved for so long, and let it sing in the present.

And I cannot do it, Lief thought, with a pang of sadness. I would not know how to begin. And even if I had the skill, it is not fitting that I should be the one.

He looked up at Tirral. Saw the longing in her glistening eyes. Suddenly knew what should be done. He held out his hands, the glowing Pipe held loosely between them.

"You are the Piper, Tirral," he said softly. "Will you play?"

✳

And so, for the first time since the world began, the pure notes of the Pirran Pipe rang out in the caverns of the secret sea, while the people of Keras listened, their rapt, upturned faces wet with tears.

The music caressed the rippling waters, echoed

from the gleaming rock, echoing, echoing until the air itself seemed to quiver with its beauty and no walls could contain it.

It flowed into the Forbidden Way, where the leeches heard it and cringed in the darkness. It sang in the opal sea, where the great eels raised their dripping heads from the water and swayed to the sound.

The Aurons building on their island looked up from their work, transfixed, as the sound drifted to their ears. Their Piper's ancient face did not change, but his body trembled all over, as if shaken by an icy gale. And Penn, packing manuscripts in her little hut on the rafts, clasped her hands in joy and wonder.

The song of the Pipe echoed through the rainbow caverns where the mud grubs burrowed deep to escape it, and the sea moles leaped and played. It filled the Glimmer with its beauty and flowed on to the ruby sea, and Plume.

Nols, tending the grave of the warrior Glock, gave a cry when she heard it. She scrambled to her feet and ran to the shore where awed, silent people were wading knee-deep, waist-deep, into the scarlet water, gazing towards the sound.

The music floated on, faint and haunting, till it reached the farthest corner of the golden sea, where Clef and Azan, fishing in their tiny boat, dropped their nets and sat spellbound. Then the last, tiny shadow of sound rose high above their heads, through the topaz haze. And carried by the cool, soft breeze, it stole into the golden dragon's enchanted sleep, bringing with it soaring dreams of sunshine, great winds and high mountains, magic and vanished glory.

4 - The Grey Zone

Tirral sat silently through the celebration that followed her playing of the Pipe. There was food, drink, and laughter around the fire, but she joined in none of it. Only when the Kerons brought out their small pipes of fungus wood did she raise her head.

The sweet, breathy music was worth listening to, indeed. And to the companions' surprise, the sweetest tunes of all were played by Emlis.

When they congratulated him, as he put down his instrument and came to sit beside his mother, Emlis bit his lip. "Playing has always brought me joy," he said. "But now I have heard the Pirran Pipe I know that the sounds I make are just a pale reflection of what music can be."

Awkwardly he wiped his pipe on his sleeve and

held it out to Barda. "Perhaps you would play for us now?" he asked. "I long to hear above-worlder music."

Barda laughed. "It is very like your own. But I am sorry, I cannot play for you — and neither can my companions. None of us is musical."

"What?"

Tirral's high-pitched exclamation cut startlingly through the music and laughter. Silence fell.

"Are you saying," cried Tirral, "that you cannot even *play* a pipe?"

"We cannot play music as you do," Lief agreed, with sinking heart. "But it is the magic of the Pirran Pipe that counts, not the skill of the player. A single note will be enough to stay the Shadow Lord's hand."

"You cannot know that!" Tirral cried. "In ancient times the Pipe was only played by Pirra's finest musicians!"

Her face glowing with renewed hope, she appealed to the silent people around her. "Our beliefs do not require us to give or lend to a cousin if the cause is pointless, Kerons! Is that not so?"

Heads nodded reluctantly.

"Well, then!" Tirral cried. "What could be more pointless than to give the Pirran Pipe to those who cannot even *play* it?" She gazed around triumphantly.

"It does not matter!"

Everyone jumped as the high, nervous voice

broke the silence. Everyone stared as Emlis stepped forward, blushing to the roots of his golden hair.

"It — it does not matter if our cousins cannot play the Pipe," Emlis stammered, meeting his mother's angry stare defiantly. "It does not matter because — because I can play very well. And I am going with them!"

✳

Much argument followed, but there was no point at all in Tirral's raging, or the companions' protesting. For the people of Keras, Emlis's announcement had removed the last objection to the Pirran Pipe's being taken to the Shadowlands.

"So you have won, and I have lost," Tirral said bitterly, as she returned the companions' weapons to them. "I have lost not only the Pirran Pipe, but my son. You have won the right to destroy them both, as well as yourselves. I hope your victory brings you joy."

Her face was ashen. The moths around her head were barely moving.

"Tirral — " Lief began. But already the Piper was turning and walking rapidly away.

"It is not *our* fault that her son is coming with us," hissed Jasmine. "It is all her own work! If she had let us go in peace Emlis would never have thought of the idea."

"Yes he would," Barda said shrewdly. "That

young man is as anxious as we are to escape this island. I think he saw his chance and seized it with both hands."

"But he does not realize what he is doing!" muttered Lief.

"No," growled Barda. "And do we?"

✳

Within hours, two longboats rowed by silent, craggy-faced leech-gatherers were setting out from the north side of the island. Lief, Jasmine, Barda, and Emlis sat in the stern of one boat. In the other were the frozen-faced Tirral and two of her closest advisors.

Green water stretched ahead, gradually darkening to grey. The horizon was shrouded in darkness.

Kree clucked uneasily.

"The Grey Zone," Jasmine said, staring at the ominous horizon.

Emlis nodded. Fear mingled with excitement on his thin face, which was almost covered by the hood of the thick, dull green leech-gatherer's cloak he wore.

"It is not too late to change your mind, Emlis," muttered Barda, who was sitting beside him. "This is not one of Doran's tales. It is real, and deadly."

"I cannot change my mind now," said Emlis. "You need me. They will not let you take the Pipe without me."

"Your skin is not fit for the world above, Emlis," whispered Jasmine, leaning forward. "The sun will burn you. The light will blind you."

Emlis shook his head stubbornly. "The cloak will protect me from the sun. And I am not the first Pirran to leave the caverns. Doran told of seven who did so, in the time of Alyss and Brosnan."

"They all died, Emlis," said Barda brutally. "They died, and never saw their homes again."

"They were killed by above-worlders, not by the sun," Emlis said, his voice trembling. "And in any case, they were Plumes, and the Plumes are as foolhardy and stupid as the Aurons are wicked."

"Plumes and Aurons are not stupid and wicked!" cried Jasmine. "They are your own people! Your kinsfolk! Far more closely related to you than we are."

The leech-gatherers who were paddling their boat turned and frowned ferociously. One made a low sound in his throat. The other bared his teeth unpleasantly. Jasmine pressed her lips together and returned their stares without flinching until at last they turned to face the front and began paddling once more.

Emlis hunched his bony shoulders. "I beg you, do not argue with me any more," he mumbled. "This is my one chance to fulfil the dearest wish of my life. To see a world that is not my own. If I die in the attempt, that is surely my choice."

Barda ran his hands through his tousled hair in despair. "Three of them," he muttered under his breath. "Three young hotheads. By the heavens, were not two bad enough?"

✳

Gradually the emerald light failed and within an hour the fleet was paddling through a grim realm of grey. They were far beyond the scope of Doran's map now. Beyond Deltora's border.

When they looked up, all they saw was swirling darkness. They knew that far above them towered the treacherous peaks that clustered behind Dread Mountain — iron-hard rock filled with dank, secret caves where hideous beasts like the giant toad Gellick thrived.

The boat was moving more slowly, and the rugged faces of the leech-gatherers had become strained and watchful.

Ahead loomed an ink-black shadow. The cavern beneath the Shadowlands.

"When are they going to leave us?" Jasmine murmured.

"We must go to the edge of the Shadow," one of the leech-gatherers said unexpectedly, without turning around. "So the Piper says. And there we stop, praise be to Keras, and send you up, to the evil place above."

"Send us up?" Lief blinked, confused. He had imagined that the Kerons were going to show them a secret way to the surface. But this sounded like . . .

"The magic of seven may not be needed for the task," said the leech-gatherer, "but we thought it best to be on the safe side. Who knows how deep the rock is, up above. For all your strange ideas, we would not want you caught midways, would we now?"

His companion chuckled grimly.

Lief felt Jasmine shudder, and knew that she had been gripped, as he had, by a nightmarish vision of being trapped in the midst of solid rock.

"Do not fear," said Emlis. "Our ancestors sent Doran to the surface without harm many times."

"That was long ago," muttered Barda, who was looking rather sick. "And I presume Doran was not sent into the Shadowlands."

"Oh, no!" Emlis agreed. "Doran always left the caverns in a place to the west of Keras. He said that in the land above, just at that spot, there was a great waterway and boats to help him make the journey home."

"The River Tor!" Lief exclaimed. "So that was how Doran did it so secretly. He would reappear in the brush below Dread Mountain. Then he would walk down to the river and wait for a boat. There would not have been so many pirates then."

"Or Ols," said Jasmine. Kree squawked nervously on her shoulder, but she did not turn to him. Her eyes were fixed on the mass of darkness looming before them.

The Shadowlands. Soon, very soon, she would be able to begin the search for Faith, her lost sister. And Lief and Barda would be beside her.

Jasmine had not forgiven Lief for trying to keep

knowledge of Faith hidden from her. But after all they had been through together since entering the caverns, her anger had lost its bitter edge. Now she felt sure that Lief had kept Faith a secret only out of a desperate wish to keep her, Jasmine, from harm.

He was wrong to deceive me, Jasmine thought. But he did it for reasons he thought were good.

Her eyes stared, unfocused, at the growing Shadow ahead. Waiting for Lief in Del was his bride-to-be — that well-read, noble Toran girl who would make a fitting queen, and one day bear a child to wear the Belt of Deltora after Lief. But Jasmine was here with Lief now. And she was his friend — his true friend.

And that is enough, Jasmine told herself. That is how it must be. For what do I know of palaces and politeness and fine clothes? Nothing at all, and nor do I want to. Lief knows that.

Filli whimpered softly beneath her collar, and she raised a hand to comfort him, unconsciously drawing her own comfort from his warmth.

"The first time Doran came to the caverns, he did not reach Keras," Emlis was chattering meanwhile to Barda. "Some Plumes found him drowning in the topaz sea. They saved him, but sent him straight back to the surface! That is how stupid Plumes are!"

He broke off and glanced guiltily at Jasmine, but she was still staring fixedly ahead.

"The Plumes thought Doran would forget what

had happened," Emlis said. "But a song they sang as they paddled their boat stayed in his head and made him remember. So he returned. And *this* time he — "

His eager voice broke off in a squeak.

Darkness had fallen like a curtain. The water surrounding them was black as night. They could see nothing. They could only hear the sound of the water lapping and the small craft that surrounded their longboat bumping together gently.

"It is time." Tirral's trembling voice floated in the darkness. "Now is the last chance for you to change your minds. Will you return with us to Keras, and safety? Lief . . . Barda . . . Jasmine . . . *Emlis*?"

There was a long pause.

"Very well." Tirral's voice was rigidly controlled now. "I have one piece of advice for you, and I urge you to attend to it, for I feel its worth in every bone of my body. Shadows have sunk deep into the soil of Pirra now. Whatever the Plumes and Aurons may think, Pirra is lost forever. It can never be re-claimed."

"We know this," Lief said. "And neither the Plumes nor the Aurons expect — "

"I have not finished," Tirral snapped, speaking over him. "Listen! The Shadow Lord's power is far greater now than when the Pipe kept him from Pirran soil. Played well or ill, the Pipe will stay his hand only for a time, and only if he is taken by surprise. Keep its magic for when it is most needed."

"We will," Lief, Barda, and Jasmine murmured together.

"There is nothing to do, then, but to wish you well," said Tirral from the darkness. "Put your arms about one another. Close your eyes. Think of nothing."

Feeling as though he was in a dream, Lief moved into the center of the boat. He knelt down on the hard, wet boards, spread his arms wide, and gripped his companions tightly. He bent his head, forced his mind to go blank.

"Good fortune, cousins." The rough voice of one of the leech-gatherers rumbled low in the silence. Then . . .

Cold, freezing cold. Rushing darkness. Sick dizziness, unbearable . . .

There was a sudden, terrifying stillness. A bleak, bitter smell. A rapid, thumping sound, very close, mingled with the moaning wail of wind. And Lief opened his stinging eyes, took his first, gasping breath, in the Shadowlands.

5 - In the Shadowlands

Lief lay very still, slowly realizing that the thumping sound he was hearing was the pounding of his own heart. He was sprawled face down on hard earth. Wind was sweeping over him, a draft that seemed neither hot nor cold, carrying with it the bitter smell he had noticed before.

Cautiously he raised his head, blinking in the sullen light. Jasmine was crouching beside him, Kree on her shoulder. Barda was crawling to his feet not far away. Emlis, swathed in his cloak, was still on the ground, curled in a small ball.

With a chill Lief realized that they were in the open, on a windswept plain pocked with gaping craters. Barren white clay, as parched and cracked as a dry riverbed, stretched in front of them as far as the eye could see. Thick grey clouds boiled low overhead, hiding the sun.

The land was dead. Dead as bleached, white bones.

Lief's eyes burned as words from *The Tale of the Pirran Pipe* sprang unbidden into his mind.

Long, long ago, beyond the Mountains, there was a green land called Pirra, where the breezes breathed magic. . . .

Pirra, once a land of beauty, sunshine, and flowers. The ancient home of the Kerons, the Plumes, and the Aurons. Now . . . this wasteland.

And this is what Deltora might have been. Still might be. If you were wrong, Lief. If you were wrong . . .

Lief shook his head, trying to shut out the voice in his mind, the tormenting voice of his own conscience. But it would not stop.

You should have let Jasmine go. You should have remained in Del. That was your duty. Your duty . . .

Jasmine was pulling at his arm. "Lief! We must take cover, quickly," she hissed. "There are — things here. Coming closer."

Lief tore his gaze from the barren horizon and looked at her. Her eyes were startled, wide, almost black.

"People? Beasts? Ols?" he asked quickly.

"I — do not know," Jasmine whispered. "Things." She shuddered. Filli whimpered in his hiding place under her jacket.

Barda had scooped Emlis from the ground and was hurrying towards them.

"Do not just stand there!" he said roughly. "If an Ak-Baba should sight us, we are finished!" He grabbed Lief by the arm and swung him around.

Only then did Lief realize that they were not marooned in the middle of the vast plain, as in his confusion he had thought. Behind them, rising like a great, jagged fence, were the mountains, their cruel peaks piercing the cloud, their foothills edging the plain. The great bulk of Dread Mountain hulked in the background, spreading away to the west.

Of course! Lief thought, sprinting towards the bare, forbidding foothills with the others pounding close behind him. The Kerons spirited us to the surface just inside the Shadowlands border. Of *course* the mountains are here! What was I thinking of?

He heard Emlis waking, protesting, demanding to be put down. Well, that was one good thing. Barda would have his hands free to climb, at least. Lief swerved around the first of the grey boulders that lay at the edge of the plain and began to scramble rapidly upward, aiming for the shelter of the larger rocks he could see farther ahead.

Then, suddenly, a white flash of pain exploded behind his eyes as something slammed against his brow with shocking force. He staggered backwards, arms spinning wildly, fighting to keep his balance. Through the ringing in his ears he heard muffled cries of alarm, then, with relief, he felt a firm hand on his back. Barda was supporting him, pushing him back on his feet.

Trembling, he sank to his knees. Barda, Jasmine, and Emlis crouched beside him, pressing closely together so that the great boulder hid them from the plain.

"Lief, what happened?" he heard Jasmine whisper.

"Did you not see?" he mumbled, pressing his hands to his aching head. "Something hit me."

"No!" she whispered back. "There was nothing there. You just jerked backwards, suddenly, for no reason. One minute you were running, the next — "

Barda drew breath sharply. He picked up some pebbles and threw them at the empty air in front of them. Astounded, Lief saw the pebbles stop short in midair, bounce slightly back, then fall to the ground.

"An invisible wall!" Jasmine breathed.

"Yes," Barda said grimly. "I thought it strange that the mountains were unprotected. The Shadow Lord has sealed the border in his own way, it seems."

As he spoke, they saw movement near where one of the pebbles had fallen. A small, brown striped lizard with bright eyes had scuttled into view.

"But it came from uphill!" whispered Jasmine excitedly. "From behind the magic wall. I saw it! Is it only humans who are stopped by the shutting spell?"

Lief felt ill. He had thought of another explanation, and he could see by Barda's grim face that Barda had thought of it, too.

The lizard's tiny forked tongue flickered in and

out for a few moments. Then, abruptly, it turned and scuttled back uphill. When it reached the invisible wall it stopped dead and fell back.

"Yes," Barda said slowly. "That is what I feared. The spell does not stop people or creatures coming in. It only prevents them getting out."

He, Lief, and Jasmine looked at one another, the words hanging heavily between them. Then Lief began struggling to rise.

"Stay still," Jasmine hissed, catching hold of his arm to hold him down. "You must rest. You hit your head — "

"No!" Lief gritted his teeth and pulled against her restraining hand.

Jasmine's grip tightened and he fell back with a groan, his head swimming. "You said — you said something was coming!" he mumbled. "We must — "

"Do as you are told for once, Lief!" said Barda grimly, drawing his sword. "We are as safe behind this rock as anywhere, at present. And whatever Jasmine can hear, I can still see nothing."

The little lizard was scrabbling frantically at the invisible wall now, running along it for a short distance, then turning and running the other way. Every now and then it would raise itself and push with its front legs at the empty air, its tail thrashing frantically.

"But — but why does the Shadow Lord not protect his border?" asked Emlis in a high, trembling voice. "He has many of your people! Does he not fear that an army — or a small group such as yours — might cross the mountains and invade his territory?"

"That is what he *hopes* for, I would say," muttered Barda. "He has left the way open, after all."

"But why?" asked Emlis, his voice rising to a squeak.

The lizard fell back, exhausted. Instantly, an orange, spiny beetle-like creature sprang from a crack in the clay just behind it. In the blink of an eye the orange creature had seized the lizard, bitten off its head, and dragged the still twitching carcass back under the earth.

"Does that answer your question?" asked Barda dryly.

Emlis stared at him, open-mouthed.

Lief turned his face to the rock, his stomach churning. Then he saw it. A mark had been scratched laboriously into the rock's hard surface. He stared, hardly able to believe his eyes.

"The sign of the Resistance!" he breathed, tracing the mark with his fingers. His heart was pounding.

Another Deltoran had sheltered here. A Deltoran who had somehow escaped from captivity and made for the mountains, only to find the way to freedom barred. A Deltoran who had used, perhaps, his or her last strength not to weep and curse fate, but to scratch a message of defiance on the rock.

The despairing confusion that had clouded Lief's mind ever since arriving in this dread place seemed suddenly to lift. Suddenly he was able to think again.

Barda was touching the sign now. "It is not fresh, but it is not very old, either," he said slowly. "A year or two at most, I think."

Lief was remembering another Resistance sign he had seen marked on rock. It had ended a message written in blood on a cave wall in Dread Mountain.

Doom had written that message: Doom, the only Deltoran captive ever known to have escaped from the Shadowlands. And he had escaped from . . .

Kree gave a low, warning squawk. "The light is changing," Jasmine whispered, reaching for her dagger.

Lief and Barda looked up quickly. The low, tumbling clouds were stained with faint, sullen scarlet, and the whiteness of the plain was dimming.

"Surely something as small as a lizard would not have sounded a border alert," Barda muttered. "Such things must happen often."

"It is the setting sun," said Lief, looking to the west, where the clouds glowed more deeply. "Night is falling."

They were silent for a moment. They had been in

the caverns so long that they had almost forgotten that the days in the world above were ruled by the movement of the sun.

"Doran said sunsets were glorious to see," said Emlis, gazing with disappointment at the clouds. "Doran said they were like red and orange fire blazing in the sky."

"Not here, it seems," Barda growled.

Jasmine was peering not at the sky, but at the plain. "Look," she breathed, pointing.

The plain was coming to life. Legs scrabbling, long feelers waving, spiny orange beetles were emerging in the thousands from the cracks in the clay.

6 - The Wild Ones

L ief looked down. The cracks in the earth near his feet were full of movement, though so far nothing had ventured to the surface.

"I do not like this," Barda said. "We had better move on. Those insects are small, but there are many of them, and they are meat-eaters. If they are hungry enough — "

He did not complete his sentence, but he had said enough to make everyone stand hastily.

"Which way?" Jasmine looked desperately left and right.

"West," Lief said instantly, turning to face the dark red glow that was the setting sun.

"Why west?" Jasmine demanded. "If we are to find the Shadow Lord's headquarters in time — "

"What?" Barda interrupted, staring at her in disbelief. "What madness is this? The Shadow Lord's *headquarters*? Why, that is the very place that we must avoid at all costs!"

"But — but the slaves!" Jasmine stammered, flushing hotly. She had betrayed herself. She had forgotten that her companions knew nothing of her plans.

She was sure that Faith was somewhere in or near the Shadow Lord's headquarters. The little girl had been secretly using something she called "the crystal" to call for help. And where could such a magical object be, except in the Shadow Lord's main stronghold? Somehow, Jasmine had to convince her companions to seek it.

Should she admit her secret at last? Tell Lief and Barda what Faith had said?

Almost immediately she decided she could not risk it. Not here, on this windswept plain, where every gust of wind brought the scent of danger. She had kept the secret too long for that. This was no place for argument, for loss of trust, for the angry words that she knew would burst forth from her as soon as they questioned her.

No, Jasmine thought. I have played a lone hand this far. I must continue doing so until the time is right.

"The slaves must be scattered all over this cursed land!" Barda was growling. "Why do you think — ?"

"Wait!" Lief suddenly looked rapidly from side to side. "Where is Emlis?"

Shocked, Jasmine and Barda swung around. Emlis was no longer behind them. He had disappeared.

"But — but he was *here*! Standing beside the rock!" spluttered Barda.

"Well he is here no longer," Lief said grimly. "He must have wandered away while we were arguing."

It was growing darker by the moment. Quickly they separated and, calling in low voices, searched the immediate area. But Emlis was nowhere to be found.

They came together again at the large boulder, all of them fearful and angry.

"I cannot believe this!" Barda ground his teeth in fury. "What game does the young fool think he is playing?"

"We will have to go on without him," Jasmine snapped, burning with impatience. "There is no time to waste. And those insects are massing in their millions!"

Lief squinted over the plain. The clay, darkened by the setting sun, was now the same color as the beetles. The insects would have been perfectly camouflaged except that they were so many. The ground seethed with them, rippling like water driven by the tide.

The ripples seemed particularly large at one spot, beside the nearest crater. It was as though waves were breaking over a large rock lying there.

My mind is still half in the secret sea, Lief thought. Then, suddenly, he leaned forward, peering intently through the gloom. Why would the beetles crowd so closely together just at that place? It was almost as if . . .

Hideous understanding shot through him like a thunderbolt. He shouted and sprang forward.

He could hear Jasmine and Barda chasing him, hissing to him to stop, as he ran out onto the plain, crushing dozens of beetles with every thud of his flying feet. But there was no time, no time to stop, to explain. No time to tell them why his stomach was heaving, his heart was racing . . .

In moments he had reached the heaving mass of beetles by the crater and was plunging his arms into its midst. Then, panting and shuddering, he was hauling the limp, bleeding body of Emlis from the ground.

Exclaiming with horror, Barda and Jasmine began beating the clinging insects from Emlis's shredded garments, and tearing them from the raw, bloody flesh beneath. Around their feet, thousands of beetles scuttled in panic, fighting one another for space as they squeezed back into the cracks in the clay.

Emlis was groaning feebly, trying to speak.

"How did this happen?" shouted Barda. "Was he so mad as to walk out — "

The words dried in his throat. His eyes bulged. As he raised his sword, Lief and Jasmine swung around to look at what he had seen.

Shapes were rising out of the crater — ragged, shambling shapes with bared teeth and glowing eyes.

Clawed hands reached for them. Low growls and piercing howls rose in a terrifying chorus of baffled anger.

Half carrying, half dragging Emlis, Lief turned and stumbled back towards the hills, beetles scattering before him. Barda and Jasmine backed after him, their weapons held in front of them to fend off the ghastly creatures crawling in ever greater numbers from the crater.

The creatures were like humans — yet hideously changed. Some were covered in hair, with fangs and tusks protruding from their gaping mouths. Some had shrunken limbs, long tails, and scaly skin. Others had humped backs covered in gleaming shell, twisted, insect-like legs, and spiny fins for arms. Roaring and howling, they began to spread out, encircling the fleeing companions like a pack of animals closing in on prey.

Lief, Barda, and Jasmine reached the rock marked with the sign of the Resistance and, speechless with horror, turned to fight. The creatures were coming at them from all sides. There would be no escape.

Then, suddenly, a shiver seemed to run through the savage horde and it stopped dead. There was a long, low rumbling like distant thunder and at the same moment the dim light brightened.

Instinctively, Lief looked up, and a cold shiver ran down his spine. Instead of the rising moon, which he had expected to see, another shape was forming in the sky. Huge and menacing it shone like cold white fire against the greyness of the clouds.

Moaning and whimpering, the creatures were falling to the ground, covering their eyes.

"Now! Run!" hissed Barda, heaving Emlis over his shoulder.

Together they left the cover of the rock, broke through the ring of creatures cringing on the ground, and began to run along the line of the hills, towards the west.

After only a few moments, they heard the sounds of pounding feet behind them and a terrible chorus of baying, grunting, and howling. The creatures had recovered from their fear at the rising of the mark of the Shadow Lord, and were in hot pursuit.

Not daring to look back, the companions raced on, swerving around boulders, stumbling over the rough ground, buffeted by the relentless wind that gusted across the plain. Then they saw, not far ahead, something barring their way. A long, rocky outcrop jutted out into the plain, gleaming in the terrible light from the sky.

"Over the top!" Barda panted. "We — cannot risk — going around it. Must not let them — get in front of us."

They reached the barrier and leaped upward, scrambling to the top and sliding down the other side.

Lief tumbled to the hard ground, jarring his shoulder painfully. As Jasmine landed beside him, he jumped to his feet and reached up to Barda, to take Emlis's weight. Then he heard Jasmine shriek his name. He swung around, clutching Emlis in his arms, and saw something that made his blood run cold.

Not far ahead of them was another outcrop, higher than the one they had just climbed. And from its shadow, something was emerging — something huge and dome-shaped that gleamed with the same dull sheen as the rocks. Its vast body rippled and bulged horribly as it moved, as though the thick, smooth skin clothed flesh that was nothing more than quivering jelly.

As it crawled farther into the light, Lief gave a strangled gasp. He heard Filli squealing in terror and Kree screeching, heard Barda's muttered curse. Ringing the beast's body like the swollen beads of a hideous necklace were dozens of heads, each one with glassy, staring eyes and a lipless mouth from which hung a long, thin, dripping tongue.

The companions flattened themselves against the

rock. The sounds of howling and pounding feet were growing louder. Their pursuers were closing in. To turn and climb back the way they had come would be to deliver themselves straight into the pack's hands.

But the beast was moving towards them. It was gliding effortlessly over the rough ground on hundreds of tiny legs that were almost hidden beneath a fringe of skin hanging from its body like a ragged skirt. Its many eyes had swivelled to fix on the intruders. Its tongues were lengthening, curling and quivering ominously.

"We must split up and try to get around it," muttered Barda to Lief and Jasmine. "You two go right. I will go left, with Emlis."

But the moment they took a step, there was a hiss and tongues shot forward like striking snakes in both directions, missing Barda and Jasmine by a hair. They shrank back against the rock. Clearly, they were not to be allowed to move.

The beast's body rippled and seemed to swell as it glided closer, its blank eyes gleaming.

7 - The Beast

Shoulder to shoulder with Barda and Jasmine, Lief faced the beast. It undulated before them, its tongues flickering and curling, its body flattening and spreading, rising slightly on the side that faced the rock.

It is preparing to engulf us, Lief thought.

His legs felt weak. His heart was pounding. His sword hand was slippery with sweat. Sweat was running down into his eyebrows, too, and as he cautiously raised his free hand to wipe it away, his arm brushed the Pirran Pipe hidden beneath his shirt. Into his mind flew the promise he had made to Tirral.

The Pipe will not be lost. It will be returned to the caverns, I swear it!

Lief licked his dry lips. That vow, it seemed, had been worthless. As worthless as *all* his promises — to the Plumes, to the Aurons, to Marilen . . .

Do not fear, Marilen. You need do nothing but wait.

The wind moaned around the rocks, like the ghostly voice of his own despair.

"The Pipe, Lief," Barda gasped beside him. "The Pipe! Use it!"

Lief hesitated. The Pipe might indeed stop the beast. It might give them a chance to escape. But the moment it was played, the Shadow Lord would become aware of it, and of them.

They would lose the advantage of surprise. They would be hunted down mercilessly, without ever finding the prisoners, let alone setting them free.

He forced himself to slide his hand under his shirt and loosen the drawstring at the top of the red cloth bag. The tips of his fingers touched the Pipe, grasped it . . .

A warm tingling ran through his hand, along his arm, through his body. It was like new blood rushing through his veins, strengthening his trembling legs, stilling his racing heart.

He straightened his shoulders, took a deep breath, suddenly alive again. Through the eerie wailing of the wind he heard the angry sounds of the pack on the other side of the outcrop.

Suddenly he knew what he must do.

"We are here!" he roared at the top of his voice. "Come and get us!"

"Lief!" screamed Jasmine in terror.

Howls and screams of rage filled the air. There

was the sound of frenzied climbing, the rattling and scrabbling of claws.

"Flatten yourself against the rock!" Lief shouted, pushing Barda and Jasmine back. "As hard as you can! Ready — "

Growling shrieks sounded above them, and the next moment savage figures were throwing themselves blindly, heedlessly, over the edge of the outcrop. Screams of triumph became shrieks of terror as the attackers realized their mistake too late. Twisting and howling they thudded down on the billowing body of the beast, puncturing its skin with claws and tusks, rolling to fall sprawling onto the clay.

Dragging Emlis with them, the companions began edging along the outcrop, towards the open plain. They began slowly and carefully, never taking their eyes from the beast. But it was no longer interested in them. Swelling and spinning, clear fluid bubbling from the gashes in its skin, it was striking out at the new intruders, at the attackers who had dared to injure it.

Hissing, a dozen tongues darted out, curling around the writhing figures on the ground. Other tongues flicked upward, reaching for the creatures still teetering on the edge of the outcrop. The tongues snatched the nearest off their feet to drag them, screaming, to their doom.

The companions had nearly reached the end of the outcrop. Now was the moment of decision. Should they run out onto the plain and risk whatever new horror might be lurking there? Or should they make for the second outcrop, which meant crossing the perilous space in which the beast still spun and hissed?

Lief looked back, and his stomach seemed to turn over. The beast's body — its torn, rippling body — was coming apart! The heads around its sides were tearing themselves away from the billowing mass, dragging great chunks of flesh with them.

Staring wild-eyed, Lief heard Barda give a choking cry, and Jasmine gasp in understanding. Then, suddenly, he, too, saw the truth. The extra heads ringing the monster's body did not belong to the monster at all. They belonged to its young — smaller versions of itself that the beast carried in pouches around its vast body.

The young were crawling away from their injured parent now, leaving gaping cavities behind them. Each one was as tall as a man, and four times as broad. Each was eager to drag in the prey it had captured with its curling tongue, and to feast.

Their ears ringing with the howls and screams of the captives as the monsters engulfed them, the companions sprinted across the gap. They reached the second outcrop, swung around it, and pelted towards the scattered boulders that marked the edge of the plain.

Panting and trembling, they took refuge behind the largest stone they could see. Emlis was moaning in pain. Barda put him down and together the companions cleaned and dressed his wounds as best they could, using ointment and bandages given to them by the Kerons.

For a long time none of them spoke of what they had just escaped. The memory of it was too raw. But at last, when Emlis lay quiet, Barda found his voice.

"I am sorry," he mumbled. "It is no thanks to me that we are safe. I thought we were finished. I could not think — could do nothing but despair. And still I feel numb. I do not know what has happened to me."

Lief glanced at Jasmine. Her face was pale and shadowed. Filli was hiding beneath her jacket, only his nose visible. Kree, his feathers ruffled, hunched on her shoulder.

"You feel it, too, Jasmine," Lief said quietly.

She nodded shortly. "I have been trying to fight it, but it is impossible," she muttered. "It is as if . . ." She swallowed painfully. ". . . as if I take in fear with every breath. As if the very air of this place is poisoned."

With a start, Lief remembered the strange, bitter smell he had noticed on the wind when first they reached the Shadowlands. He had grown accustomed to it, and had not thought about it for a long time. But now he realized that Jasmine had hit upon the truth. The wind was the Shadow Lord's way of sapping the will of those who entered his realm. The bitter scent it carried was the stink of despair.

"You are right!" he exclaimed. "But we *can* fight

it." He pulled out the red cloth bag. Carefully he slid the Pipe from its casing and held it out to Barda and Jasmine. As they clasped it, he could see their faces change. The strange, hopeless expressions disappeared, their eyes brightened, their mouths grew firm.

"Why — it is miraculous!" breathed Barda.

"See if it will help Emlis, too!" Jasmine urged.

They placed the Pipe between Emlis's pale fingers. And sure enough, after only a few moments the young Keron's eyes flickered open. He stared up at the companions in bewilderment, then gave a start and struggled to sit up. The Pipe began to slip to the ground. Lief grabbed it before it fell, and put it back into the red cloth bag.

"Where are we?" Emlis was gabbling. "What happened? The creatures . . . they seized me, carried me, and then — " His eyes widened with horror as full memory flooded into his mind.

"Stay still, Emlis," said Lief quickly, tucking the red bag inside his shirt once more. "Gather your strength. We must move on very soon."

"Indeed," Barda muttered, glancing over his shoulder at the outcrop, which was still too near for comfort. All was silent behind the outcrop now. Lief repressed a shudder. He did not want to think about what was happening there.

Jasmine was also looking back, but for a different reason. "Our way to the east is barred now, unless we want to risk crossing the beast's territory once more," she said, frowning. "Why were you so intent on moving west, Lief?"

Lief leaned forward, eager to explain. "Because I remembered Doom," he said. "Doom escaped from the Shadow Arena. From there he went straight through the hills into Deltora, and was pursued up Dread Mountain by the Grey Guards. So . . ."

"So the Arena must be very near the border — and near the western slopes of Dread Mountain!" exclaimed Barda. "Yes! Why did I not think of it? If we keep moving west, we should find it easily."

"And surely the Shadow Arena must be where many of the prisoners are," said Lief, turning to Jasmine. "If they are to be put to death as the bird told you . . ."

He paused, and Jasmine nodded uneasily. It had not been a bird, but Faith, who had told her that the prisoners were in danger.

It does not matter, she told herself. The truth is the truth, whoever tells it.

Barda clambered to his feet. "West it is, then," he said. "Not that we have a choice. I, for one, do not wish to cross that beast's path again." He glared at Jasmine, daring her to disagree.

But Jasmine had been thinking rapidly. Lief was right. The Shadow Arena had to be near the border, and near Dread Mountain, too. And she had remembered something else. Poison for the Grey Guards' deadly blister weapons had been carried through a pass that led from Dread Mountain into the Shadowlands.

No one would move glass jars of lethal poison any farther than necessary. So almost certainly the factory where the blisters had been made was close to the pass, on the Shadowlands side.

The Shadow Arena *and* the factory. Both very important sites. Both near Dread Mountain. It made perfect sense for one of the Shadow Lord's main bases, at least, to be in the same place. And Faith, perhaps, very near.

She bowed her head so that Barda would not see the flash of hope in her eyes. "Very well," she murmured. "If you think it right, we will continue moving west."

Barda frowned at her suspiciously. Jasmine was not usually so agreeable. But he did not waste time in questioning her. He was already helping Emlis to his feet, anxious to be gone.

Lief stood beside them and peered out onto the plain. It was flooded with light, but no moon, no stars could be seen through the thick cloud. The mark of the Shadow Lord dominated the sky, burning with cold white fire.

"We will have to go carefully," he murmured, turning to look at the ragged line of rocks that straggled away to the west. "There is little cover. If we are seen — "

"You have been seen already, you fool!" croaked a harsh voice at his feet. And before he could move or speak, claws had seized his ankles, and were dragging him down.

8 ~ Claw

Scrabbling helplessly at the hard earth, Lief felt the scrape of stone on his legs. With a surge of panic he realized that he was being dragged feet-first into a hole that had opened beneath the rock.

Desperately he flung his arms forward. Gasping with shock, Jasmine, Emlis, and Barda seized them, trying in vain to hold him back. He tried to kick, but the scaly talons that gripped his ankles merely tightened their hold and pulled more strongly. He felt as if he was being torn in two. He yelled in pain and terror.

"Shut your mouth or you will kill us all!" barked the harsh voice.

There were grunts and curses from below. Then, suddenly, Lief felt another pair of hands seize his legs and heave. His arms slipped from his companions' grasp, and he slithered under the rock, falling with a thud onto hard ground.

Instantly he was lifted up and slammed against a wall, a vast hand around his throat. Dazed, half-strangled, he saw that the rock had not been a loose boulder at all, but part of the roof of a large cave. A torch flickered on rocky walls and floor. Water trickled in the shadows. A small group of strangely ill-assorted beings was peering at him.

There was a bearded scarecrow of a man whose hands were scaly claws, like the talons of a bird of prey. Beside him stood a woman — young and tall but gaunt with sunken eyes, the brand of the Shadow Lord burned cruelly into her brow. And pinning Lief to the wall, scowling, filthy, with an iron band around his neck, was — Glock!

Lief gaped at the brutish face snarling so close to his own. This could not be! He was dreaming! Glock was dead — dead and buried in a hero's grave on the island of Plume. Had an Ol taken the shape of Glock to deceive them? A Grade 3 Ol, that could mimic even the warm touch of a human being?

But if that was so, surely the Ol would pretend to recognize him, would greet him by name, in Glock's voice. No flicker of recognition showed in this man's eyes.

The enormous paw around Lief's throat tightened as Jasmine thudded through the hole in the cave roof, with Barda and Emlis close behind. His companions' weapons were in their hands. They sprang forward, then saw Lief pinned against the wall and froze.

"Move another step and I will snap his neck like a twig!" growled the being who looked like Glock.

"Put down your weapons," snapped the talon-handed man, stepping forward. "We are friends!"

"You may call dragging our companion into this place the act of a friend, but we do not," growled Barda, raising his sword a little.

The man put his head on one side and regarded him curiously. "Brianne, close the trapdoor!" he ordered over his shoulder.

Frowning furiously the tall woman went to do his bidding. "You were a fool to bring them here, Claw!" she said sharply, as the light in the cave abruptly darkened. "Did I not tell you?"

"Was I to leave them to the Wild Ones?" the talon-handed man drawled. "You were glad enough to be saved when *you* were wandering the plain, Brianne. I tell you, I heard them talking! They are harmless."

The being who looked like Glock spat disgustedly. "Harmless? You are mad! At best they are decoys, at worst, spies. Look at them! Do they look like escaped slaves? They show no sign of the Sadness."

"And they came from the east, Claw," Brianne exclaimed. "All the slaves are in the west. With our own eyes we saw them trekking across the plain, chained together and under heavy guard, with Ak-Baba flying overhead. With our own ears we heard the guards taunting them, telling them they were going to the Shadow Arena. How could these four have escaped?"

Jasmine drew a sharp breath. Lief could imagine what she was thinking, and it was all he could do to keep his own face expressionless. He had been right. All the slaves were being herded into the Arena. Some terrible plan was afoot. They had to get away from here, and quickly.

Lief met Barda's eyes and blinked. Barda's mouth tightened very slightly.

"Well, strangers?" Claw said crisply. "You have heard my friends' opinions. Explain yourselves!"

"We do not have to explain ourselves to you," Lief gasped. "We do not desire your help or your company. We merely wish to go on our way."

"Indeed!" said Claw, bowing mockingly. "And why should we allow you to do that?"

In seconds he had his answer, for before he could blink Barda had sprung forward, and Barda's sword was at his throat.

A strangled groan burst from Lief as the powerful hand that gripped his neck tightened viciously.

Barda merely smiled. "Will it be a life for a life, then?" he asked Claw casually. "I can well do without the lad, who is far more trouble than he is worth. Can your friends do without you?"

Lief's attacker growled angrily. Brianne, stone-faced, folded her arms to conceal her trembling.

"Your point is well made," said Claw, apparently

entirely unmoved. He raised his voice. "Let the boy go!"

Lief felt the choking grip slacken. Then his captor stepped away from him. Lief slid down to the cave floor, points of light dancing before his eyes, the breath rasping in his bruised throat. As Emlis and Jasmine ran to him, Barda pushed Claw over to join them.

The other cave-dwellers faced them, not daring to move.

"I fear our relationship has started badly," said Claw calmly, as if he was in conversation at a polite social gathering. "This is a pity, for I think we will have to help one another, very soon. You do not act like escaped slaves, certainly. But I do not think you are Shadow Lord creatures either."

"What are they then?" snapped Brianne. Then, suddenly, her hand flew to her mouth and her eyes widened.

Claw nodded, without taking his eyes from Barda. "They are proof of what I said the day the red clouds swept back over the mountains and the Wild Ones screamed and trembled at the Enemy's fury. Deltora is free. Somehow the Belt of Deltora has been restored, and the heir to its power found. Our visitors have come across the mountains from Deltora."

Barda's face remained expressionless.

The corner of Claw's mouth twitched with something like amusement. "You do not trust us," he said.

"Perhaps things will improve if we introduce ourselves. I am known as Claw, for reasons that must be plain. My real name, however, is Mikal, of Del."

He saw Lief's eyes widen, saw Jasmine and Emlis glance swiftly at his talons. He smiled without humor.

"You are surprised," he remarked. "Did you think I was some strange oddity from a land far away? Oh, no, my friends. I am a citizen of Del — or was, before Deltora forgot me. I lived and worked at the pottery. Perhaps you know it?"

He waited, and receiving no response, went on. "When I came here with my family, the Enemy made some — improvements — to my appearance. The Enemy enjoys such . . . experiments."

He stretched out his talons and flexed them thoughtfully. "These are strong, and serve me well," he said. "I escaped the Factory before the Enemy had quite finished with me. I am one of the lucky ones. Others are not so fortunate. Your small companion in the hood has already met some of them on the Dead Plain, I think, when they used him as Scuttler bait. We call them the Wild Ones."

He smiled grimly.

Lief heard Emlis whimper softly, felt Barda tense, and Jasmine's hand seek his own. Sick with horror, he stared at Claw, forcing himself to face the terrible truth. The savage creatures who had stolen Emlis — those hideous half-beast, half-human beings who prowled the arid plain — were his own people. Maddened, hopeless victims of the Shadow Lord's evil.

Satisfied by the effect of his words, Claw waved his hand at the tall woman. "Brianne is the newest member of our group." His mouth twisted in a mocking half smile. "Often do I regret the day I brought her in. She is as stubborn as a donkey, and has been a thorn in my side from the first."

The tall woman glared and straightened her shoulders. "Brianne of Lees," she said abruptly.

A memory tweaked at Lief's mind. Brianne of Lees. Where had he heard that name before?

But Claw was speaking again. "Brianne escaped from the Shadow Arena. Only the third Deltoran ever to have done so, it is said. What happened to the first, I do not know. But the second is here."

He gestured towards the hulking figure scowling beside Brianne. "This is the last member of our party. The last, and greatest, according to his own account. Gers, of the Jalis."

"Gers!" Jasmine burst out, staring.

The man Claw had called Gers stuck out his jaw and clenched his enormous fists. "You find the name amusing?" he growled. "Fight me, then, weakling, and see if you are still smiling when the fight is done!"

"There is nothing wrong with your name!" Jasmine cried. "It is just that — that you look like — exactly like — a . . . a friend of ours."

"A Jalis called Glock," added Barda, never moving his sword from Claw's throat.

Gers's face grew very still. "I had a brother called Glock," he said slowly.

"Do not listen to them, Gers!" Brianne exclaimed. "They are the Enemy's creatures! They are trying to deceive you!"

Gers's eyes narrowed. "I will not be deceived. I *had* a brother. He was one year my elder. But he is long dead. I saw him struck down on the field of battle when the Jalis made their last stand against the Enemy. Just before — before we were taken." His huge hand moved to finger the iron collar around his neck.

"Glock may have been struck down, but he did not die," Jasmine said, very moved. "He lived to play a great part in forcing the Shadow Lord from Deltora, and died a hero's death in — "

Barda cleared his throat and Jasmine broke off, realizing that she had nearly said too much.

" — in — in our arms," she finished lamely. As Gers frowned suspiciously, she quickly slipped Glock's talisman from around her neck and held it out to him.

"Glock gave this to me, just before he died," she said. "Do you know what it is?"

Gers's eyes widened. "Our family's talisman!" he mumbled, his lips barely moving as he stared at the small, faded bag. "The wooden charm of a goblin killed by one of our ancestors. A stone from the belly of a Diamond Serpent, and two more from a dragon's nest. Herbs of great power. And the flower of a Gripper. Never did I think to see it again."

Jasmine glanced at Lief and Barda. Her face showed that she, at least, was convinced. Again she held out her hand to Gers.

"Take it," she urged softly. "It is yours by right, and Glock would want you to have it. He gave it to me because there was no one else, and we had fought side by side. It is no longer complete, I fear, for the thing you call the charm of the goblin is gone. But perhaps you will be glad to have it, in any case."

The big man stared, still making no move to take the little bag. "What did Glock say when he gave you this?" he muttered.

"He said — " Jasmine's voice trembled slightly, but she clenched her fists and continued. "He said, 'You have the heart of a Jalis. Take my talisman from my neck. It is yours now. May it serve you well.' "

Gers wet his lips. " '*Take my talisman from my neck. It is yours now. May it serve you well,*' " he repeated. "Those are the words! The words that are always said when the talisman is passed on."

He turned to Claw. "She speaks the truth!" he said, his rough voice husky with emotion. "She bore arms with my brother. And if he said she has the heart of a Jalis, she does indeed."

He faced Jasmine again, bowed low, and took the

talisman from her hand. "One day, I hope, there will be a time when I, too, will bear arms with you," he said. Clearly it was the greatest compliment he could offer.

Jasmine smiled. "Then leave this place now, and journey with us to the west, Gers," she said in a low voice. "The time has come."

9 ~ West

Within the hour, the companions were moving westward once more. But they were not travelling overland, in the way they had expected. They were crawling through a tunnel below the earth. And they were no longer alone. Not only Gers, but Claw and Brianne, too, were with them.

Lief was glad enough of the cave-dwellers' help and their company, but he had not expected it. The cave-dwellers still did not even know their visitors' names. After her dramatic announcement, all Jasmine had told Gers was that she and her friends were intent on freeing the slaves in the Shadow Arena.

She had said nothing of the Pirran Pipe, so the quest sounded foolhardy indeed. Lief understood that it might appeal to Gers, but he had expected Claw and Brianne to be more cautious. There was something, however, that Lief had not considered.

Claw said flatly that the cave was no longer safe.

"You will not admit that you have come freshly from Deltora, my friends, but I am sure you have," he said. "You have passed through the shutting spell that guards the mountains. The Enemy has been alerted. At any moment Grey Guards will be here in swarms, sniffing you out. The sooner we leave here, the better."

Gers merely grunted agreement, but Brianne's face filled with angry despair as she turned away to fill a water bag.

His face filled with pity, Emlis drew Lief, Barda, and Jasmine aside.

"Why can we not tell Claw that his fears are groundless because we came to the Shadowlands from below?" he whispered.

"That must be told to no one!" Lief whispered back. "However all this ends, the Shadow Lord must not learn of the caverns. Your people must not be betrayed."

"But we can trust Claw and the others, I am sure of it!" Emlis hissed. "They would not tell."

"They may not tell willingly," Barda agreed grimly. "But whether they come with us or stay here, they could be captured at any time. There are many ways of making a captive speak, and the Shadow Lord knows all of them."

Emlis looked horrified.

"That is why I told Gers so little," Jasmine murmured. "The less others know of our business, the safer we will be. And the safer *they* will be also, Emlis, for what they do not know, they cannot be forced to tell."

She glanced at Lief, surprised that he had not yet spoken. Lief's head was bowed. He seemed to be in the grip of some strong feeling.

"Do you not agree, Lief!" she demanded.

"Of course," he said, looking up and meeting her eyes. "We could relieve our own minds by burdening these people with our secret. But if we do, we could be condemning them to die despising themselves for betraying their friends and their country. We must keep silent. But I agree with Emlis. It is hard."

Before Jasmine could answer, Gers lumbered past them and disappeared into the shadows at the back of the cave. Claw followed with the torch. The companions heard the grating sound of moving rock. Then, as Claw held the torch high, they saw that Gers had moved a large stone aside to reveal a small, dark tunnel.

"This tunnel leads to another Resistance cell, further west," said Claw. "We have not used it since the day of the Shadow Lord's wrath, but it will be safer than the surface."

He saw the companions hesitate, and raised his eyebrows. "We will go first, if you wish," he said.

"Gers and Brianne first," said Barda. "You, Claw, between us."

Claw nodded shortly and ushered Gers and Brianne into the tunnel. Clearly they were used to it, for they entered without hesitation. Jasmine went next, then Emlis and Barda. When it was Claw's turn, he took a last look around the cave and smiled bitterly.

"When I came to this place, it was a mere hollow under the rock, just large enough for me to hide in like a wounded animal," he said softly. "Then I heard water trickling below. Mad with thirst, I dug. I found the cave, and the water. The water comes underground from Deltora — from Dread Mountain, I think — for it fights the Shadowlands despair we call the Sadness. This place has been a refuge to me for a long time."

"I am sorry we have been the cause of your leaving it," Lief muttered, his conscience pricking him.

Claw's smile broadened. "There is nothing to be sorry for. As soon as I saw the mines being abandoned and our people herded west, I knew that the time for hiding was at an end for me. While I could pretend that hiding served a purpose — pretend that saving a few people or killing a few Guards struck a blow against the Enemy — I could bear it. Now . . ."

He extinguished the torch, and followed Barda, with Lief close behind him.

✳

The tunnel was dark and narrow. Claw's people spoke little, and on the seemingly endless journey through cramped, musty blackness there was plenty of time for Lief to wonder if they were being led into a trap.

But at last the forward movement stopped. There

was another grating sound as a stone blocking the tunnel was heaved aside. Then a long, low groan echoed back through the tunnel.

"What is it?" Lief heard Brianne whisper. "Gers!"

There was no answer. The forward movement began again as first Brianne, then those following her, joined Gers in the cave beyond the stone.

Lief heard a muffled cry, a torrent of whispers, then — nothing. With a feeling of dread, he crawled through the narrow opening after Claw.

No one had lit a torch, but the cave was not dark. Cold white light streamed through its roof, which had been broken open like an eggshell. A thick layer of dust covered the remains of a few pathetic possessions scattered on the floor. Charred bedding. A broken bowl. Some scraps of clothing.

The Shadow Lord's mark had been burned onto a rock wall spattered with blood.

It was clear what had happened here. Discovery. Attack. The very air seemed to reek of fear.

Lief moved stiffly to Barda, Jasmine, and Emlis, who were standing motionless under the hole in the roof near the burned remains of a rough ladder.

"Hellena," moaned Brianne, falling to her knees and pressing a tattered blue shawl to her cheek in an agony of grief. "Pi-Ban. Tipp. Moss. Pieter. Alexi . . ."

Claw's thin lips were pressed together. He was so still that he seemed scarcely to be breathing.

Gers spat on the mark of the Shadow Lord. "It is

fortunate for us that the Guards were too busy destroying to make a search," he muttered. "They did not find the tunnel. The rock was still in place."

"That does not mean they did not find it," Claw said grimly. "This plainly happened months ago, but they may still be waiting up above, like cats at a mouse hole."

Brianne stood up, tall and straight, her gaunt, scarred but still beautiful face icy cold. "I hope they are," she said, and her fingers caressed the dagger at her belt.

It was then that Lief suddenly remembered where he had heard her name before. It had been on the road to Rithmere. Brianne of Lees had been spoken of as a great athlete, a Champion of the Rithmere Games. It was said that she had gone into hiding, to avoid sharing the wealth she had won with her village.

That story had been false. Wickedly false, for it had made her own people hate her, as no doubt she had been told by Guards only too eager to cause suffering. Lief wished he could tell her that her people now knew what had happened to her, and mourned her loss. But he could not speak. Not yet.

Jasmine murmured to Kree, who fluttered up to the hole in the roof. They saw the bird's black shape outlined against the sky, yellow eye gleaming. Then Kree flew back to Jasmine's shoulder and gave a series of low squawks. Jasmine's face grew alert.

Gers cursed under his breath and felt for his talisman. "Do you see that?" Lief heard him mutter to Claw. "The bird is speaking to her!"

"So it seems." Claw's keen eyes regarded Jasmine and Kree with interest.

"Kree can see no Guards," Jasmine said. "But there is a large building a little to the west."

"That is the Factory," said Claw. "We must pass it to reach the Shadow Arena." His voice was low and even, but as he spoke a nerve twitched beside his eye and he unconsciously flexed his talons.

Gers glanced at him. "Better that we begin while it is still night, then," he growled.

Claw nodded shortly. Then, without another word, he strode to stand under the hole in the roof and jumped, catching the rim of the hole with his talons and hauling himself up into the open air.

Jasmine, Barda, Lief, and Brianne followed, immediately turning to catch and lift Emlis as he was heaved upward by Gers. Gers himself came last, grunting and swearing with the effort, enormous hands grabbing for support, heavy legs kicking against the cave wall.

When finally he lay grumbling on the cracked clay, the companions were free to turn west, to look their fill at the long, dark mass that hulked in the distance.

The Factory sprawled almost to the mountains'

edge. Flame belched from its tall, thin chimneys, turning the boiling cloud above to scarlet. The very sight of it filled Lief with dread.

He turned to Jasmine and saw that she was staring fixedly at the shape ahead, her green eyes calculating, her mouth set with determination. Lief felt a stirring of unease. Why would Jasmine look like that?

They began walking in single file, keeping low, moving quickly through the open spaces between the scattered rocks. The chimney flames ahead leaped high, guiding their way. Their ears strained for sounds of danger, but all they could hear was a dull, low rumble that grew louder and louder with every step they took.

The flames grew closer. The rumbling sound grew more penetrating, till the air seemed to tingle with it, and the very earth under their feet seemed to vibrate. A ghastly sweet-sour smell gusted towards them on the wind.

Now Lief could see the brutal shape of the Factory, very close. He could see a broad road running beside it, leading west, then disappearing around a great hill. He could also see the source of the terrible odor. Enormous, shadowy mounds of garbage lay between the road and the mountains.

"Those mounds will give us good cover," Barda muttered to Lief.

Claw turned. His face was gleaming with sweat.

His eyes were glassy. His lips were fixed in a smile that looked more like a sneer. "Good cover," he repeated. "Oh, yes. I found them so."

Then, abruptly, his eyes widened. "Gers! Brianne!" he cried harshly.

Lief spun around and saw, leaping towards them, a monstrous green man-shape with massive bowed shoulders, clawed hands, and a lashing tail. The creature's snake-like scales gleamed, its hideous lipless mouth split in a savage grin, its orange eyes burned.

Lief knew what it was. He had seen its like before, on Dread Mountain. It was the Shadow Lord's creation, bred to fight. The ultimate killing machine. A vraal.

10 – The Mounds

The vraal's terrible curved, knife-like claws were spread. Its tail lashed and broken clay sprayed up behind its cloven hoofs as it sprang forward. In seconds it would be upon them.

"Run, girl!" roared Gers to Jasmine. "Do not try to fight it!"

Jasmine did not need the warning, any more than Lief and Barda did. They had tried to fight a vraal once, and once was enough. This beast gloried in battle. It cared nothing for pain, did not know the meaning of fear or retreat.

Jasmine turned and ran, making for the garbage heaps. Grabbing Emlis between them, Lief and Barda pounded after her.

Hissing with fury because its opponents would not stand and fight, the vraal gave chase. The rusty broken chain that still swung from its iron collar rattled and clinked, but the vraal did not mind that. It was used to the sound. It had lived with it ever since it had escaped from captivity.

To the vraal, the sound of the broken chain represented freedom.

Freedom to kill and feed where and when it liked, instead of at the bidding of its masters.

Freedom to prowl the plain, so open, so different from the narrow confines of its cell beneath the Shadow Arena.

Freedom to prey on the man-beasts who ate scuttling beetles, the ragged slaves who dug in the holes in the earth and the grey masters who tasted bad, but who gave reasonable sport before they sank screaming under claws and teeth.

These enemies were different. The vraal could tell by their scent as well as their actions that they were not the same as the enemies it had been forced to fight of late. Fresh, rich blood still ran through their veins. Fire still burned in their hearts.

These were enemies worth killing. They were like the enemies in the old days of the Shadow Arena, strong and alive, brought in fresh every day to fight and die.

But these enemies were not fighting. They were running. Running into the hills that stank like the long-dead meat the vraal ate only when it was starving.

The vraal's nose was keen and delicate. It disliked vile smells as much as any human. It also knew that its hoofs, well fitted for almost every other surface, would not serve it well on the loose, crumbling mounds. But it hesitated only for a split second before bounding forward into the muck.

Its enemies could only hide for so long. In the end, it would find them. Soon it would be light, and the building that hunched beside the vile hills — the building that belched fire — offered no refuge. The vraal knew from experience that humans would rather die than enter it.

※

The cave-dwellers had scattered, burrowing into the mounds until they were invisible. Years of hiding had taught them to go underground immediately when threatened. Barda, Emlis, Lief, and Jasmine, however, had not been so quick. And now they could hear the vraal slipping and scrabbling close behind them.

With Jasmine in the lead, they stumbled through the dimness, often sinking knee-deep in vile, oozing waste, trying to put as much distance as possible between themselves and the beast before they attempted to stop and hide. But the vraal's sounds were growing louder. Instead of falling behind, it was drawing closer.

Then, suddenly, as they plowed around the side of a hill, the Factory loomed before them, windowless and grim.

Jasmine has led us the wrong way! Lief thought,

panic-stricken. How has this happened? Jasmine has always been able to find her way, even in the dark, and she did not hesitate for a moment. It is as though she *wants* us near the Factory. But that cannot be!

At that moment Emlis caught sight of the Factory also, squeaked, missed his footing, and slipped, cannoning into Barda.

The big man staggered, his feet digging deeply into the side of the hill. The loose surface began to slide. Then a whole section of the hill broke away. The companions were swept helplessly down with a mass of tumbling refuse to land, shocked and winded, on top of a low mound right beside the roadway.

Half covered, almost overwhelmed by the stench, they lay motionless, terrified to move.

Lief could no longer hear the vraal. Cautiously he cleared mess from his face, slid his eyes sideways, looked up, and saw it. It had climbed to the top of a mound just beyond the one that had collapsed. It was standing motionless, a fearsome silhouette against the paling sky, peering down, searching for signs of movement.

"I smell ticks!"

Lief's heart seemed to stop. The slurring voice had come from right beside his ear. He forced himself to turn his head.

A ghastly face was lying close to his own. A white-eyed face that seemed half-melted, its features blurred and twisted. As Lief recoiled in horror, the lopsided mouth grinned hideously and words dribbled from it again.

"Deltoran ticks! Do you hear me, Carns?"

Lief heard Jasmine's sharp gasp and Emlis's high, panic-stricken whimpering, which was quickly muffled, probably by Barda's hand.

"Stay still!" hissed Barda. "It cannot hurt us. Do you not see? It is half dead."

"Ticks, yes, Carn 2," croaked another voice, very near.

"The Perns claim them!" This time the voice was bubbling from below Lief's shoulder blade. "The Perns will kill the ticks and please the master. He'll see we're good for more years yet."

Something moved on Lief's chest. His stomach heaved as he saw that it was a hand, a fumbling hand with bloated fingers overflowing from the arm of a stained grey uniform.

Then, suddenly, there was movement beneath him and all around him, and it was as if his eyes suddenly cleared and he saw for the first time what surrounded him, what lay thick below him. The mound was a mass of bodies in grey uniforms, piled one on top of the other.

Sagging, misshapen heads nudged upward. Feet spilling from split boots jerked helplessly. Sprawled, flabby limbs twitched. Dissolving hands flapped and scrabbled. And slurred voices rose in a hideous, mumbling chorus. "Kill the ticks! Get them and please the master! Show the master we are not . . ."

The vraal's head twisted towards the sound, the movement. Its burning eyes seemed to flash. Its mouth split like a red, gaping wound studded with white teeth.

As it leaped forward, Lief, Jasmine, Barda, and Emlis sprang up, tearing themselves free of the feebly grasping hands, which were trying to hold them back. Kree swooped, stabbing with his powerful beak at a Guard reaching blindly for Jasmine's ankle.

"Black bird! Report — black bird and girl!" rasped the Guard. The cry was taken up by his neighbors and whispered over the mounds, echoing horribly from hundreds of dry throats. *Black bird, black bird and girl . . . report to the master, the master . . .*

Breath rasping in their chests, sick with fear and horror, the companions stumbled down to the road and began to run.

Glancing over his shoulder, Lief saw that the vraal had reached the mound from which they had just escaped. The mound was still heaving with the movement of the dying Guards. The vraal was standing at the top, its tail lashing, its claws extended.

Lief knew that the beast was relishing the moment, looking forward to the chase, the kill, the certain victory. In seconds it would be upon them. In seconds . . .

"Lief!" Jasmine shrieked.

Lief looked ahead. Jasmine was standing in front of a metal door in the Factory wall. She was holding it open. Barda and Emlis were already hurrying inside.

With a roar the vraal sprang. Before it had hit the ground, Lief was pounding towards the door. He reached it, shoved Jasmine inside, leaped after her, and swung the door shut just as the vraal crashed against it.

The companions stood panting, their backs to the door, as the beast threw itself against the metal, hissing and roaring. They were in a square room with closed doors on all sides. One of the doors, the one to their right, bore a large, black-painted symbol.

Jasmine ran to the door, pressed her ear against it, and listened intently.

Lief looked around him. There was nowhere to hide. The room was completely empty. The walls were hard, smooth, gleaming white. The ceiling shone with cold light that seemed to have no source.

Like Fallow's chamber in the palace, Lief thought. Instantly he cursed himself, and tried to block his mind.

Too late. Already memories of that other gleaming white room were flashing through his mind, bringing with them weakness and terror. He felt cold sweat break out on his forehead. He fought the memories back.

It was no use. His brain was seething with pictures, with sounds.

Alone and in secret, trusting in the protection of the Belt of Deltora, he had tried with all his might to destroy the dangerous, evil thing Fallow's chamber contained.

It had been a desperate, agonizing battle. He had fought it alone, as he knew he had to do, and he had lost. In the end, exhausted, weak, and sickened, he had had to be content with having the room bricked up and setting guards to prevent anyone entering its hallway. Then he had tried to wipe it from his mind, forget it existed.

But he could not forget. The knowledge of the core of darkness that lay hidden in the palace's heart continued to torment him.

He never spoke of it. Only one person knew what he had been through in that sealed room, and that was Marilen, for there could be no secrets between them.

Marilen. . . . Into Lief's mind swam an image of the girl as he had last seen her — shivering, wrapped tightly in her cloak, her fearful face raised to his as she bade him farewell.

He clung to the image. Clung to it like a lifeline,

using it to pull himself free of the swirling mass of fears and memories that threatened to engulf him.

He realized that Jasmine was tugging at his arm. Whispering to him urgently. Something about hiding. About —

There was a mighty crash, and the metal of the door bulged inward as the vraal thudded against it once more.

"Lief! Guards are coming!" Jasmine panted, as Filli squeaked frantically on her shoulder. She dragged Lief towards the door that bore the black symbol. It was open, and Barda and Emlis were already slipping through it into the room beyond.

"There is no one in there," Jasmine gabbled. "And I think the sign means it is forbidden to Grey Guards. That might give us some time. Make haste!"

Now Lief, too, could hear thudding footfalls and shouting voices coming towards them from somewhere deep in the building. He hurtled through the open door, with Jasmine close behind him.

11 - The Factory

As Jasmine pushed the door shut, Lief stood with Barda and Emlis staring, amazed, at the vast hall they had entered. It was as hard white and as brilliantly lit as the room they had just left, but it was far, far larger. It was filled with a low humming drone and a slow, thick, bubbling, popping sound, like the sound of cooking porridge. The air was slightly steamy and very warm, and there was a strange odor that reminded Lief a little of the smell of hot iron.

The room was filled with long metal containers on short legs. The containers were neatly spaced, one behind the other, and each stretched almost all the way across the room. From the door, Lief could not see what was inside them.

He took a step towards the closest one, then

froze. Heavy boots had pounded into the room on the other side of the door. Rough voices were shouting.

"The door's bent. Something's been trying to get in. A gang of Wild Ones, no doubt. Get a look, Bak 3."

There was the sound of the metal door unlatching. Then there was a yell and a thundering crash as the door was slammed shut again.

"Vraal!" several voices shouted amid the shuddering thumps and bangs of the beast attacking the door again.

Amazingly, the Guards still had not caught the companions' scent, and had not guessed that the vraal was pursuing intruders. Lief felt Jasmine touch his arm. She put her finger to her lips and beckoned. Then slowly, very quietly, she began to move farther into the room.

"It's not going to go away!" shouted a voice from the other side of the door. "Call the Perns!"

"No! We can handle it on our own!" another voice objected. "We have the new sparking rods, haven't we? Now's our chance to use them!"

The Guards were still concentrating on the vraal.

When they have driven it away we can escape, Lief thought. But Jasmine is right to move. We are too exposed standing here. We must find a safe place to hide while we wait.

He tiptoed after Jasmine, with Barda, who was half-carrying Emlis, following closely.

But as they reached the first of the metal containers, they all stopped dead. The container was divided into ten separate sections. Inside each compartment was what looked like a thick, slowly bubbling soup. The stuff was greyish white in color, and filled with strangely shaped lumps.

"What *is* this?" Barda muttered, wrinkling his nose.

"It does not matter," whispered Jasmine, dodging around the corner of the container and moving on. "Do not stop. There is a door at the back of the room. Let us — "

Her hand flew to her mouth and she made a choking sound.

Lief hurried to her side with Barda and Emlis. And when he saw what Jasmine had seen, his stomach turned over.

The compartments in the second tray were half full of the simmering grey-white soup. But floating in the liquid were smooth, grey, featureless objects with heads, bodies, arms, legs . . .

Barda cursed under his breath. Emlis hid his face in his hands. Jasmine's face was distorted with horror. "Dead people!" she choked. "Dead bodies dissolving . . ."

"No!" Lief had been moving along the tray, and he had seen what the others had not. Two words engraved on the metal side.

CARN POD

"They are not dissolving," he said huskily, as he moved back to his friends. "They are *forming*. These are Grey Guards. They are not born, but *grown*! Here, in the Factory!"

He stabbed a shaking finger back towards the engraved words. "We know that Grey Guards are always in groups of ten. Ten identical brothers, with the same name, who work and fight together. Do you not see? Every one of these trays is a pod! This is the Carn Pod."

Barda gritted his teeth. "The Carns are out in the garbage mound, Lief! How could they be here also?"

"Because — " Lief began.

Then, suddenly, the door at the back of the room began to open.

Like a flash, the companions crouched behind the container.

". . . just a wild vraal, it seems," a young woman's voice said. "The Baks will take care of it."

"Or *it* will take care of *them*," an older male voice sneered in reply. "The present Baks are already ten days past their fail date. They are starting to make mistakes. And even without that, the Bak model was never up to standard, in my opinion."

Footsteps sounded on the hard floor. Peering through the legs of the containers, Lief saw two pairs of white-booted feet pacing slowly across the back of the room, inspecting the last row of compartments. He also saw that the door had not swung shut, but still hung half-open.

"These new Baks are almost ready," the woman said gently, after a moment. Her voice seemed familiar to Lief, but surely that was impossible. She was clearly a Shadow Lord servant.

"Not before time," the man snapped. "I told you! Guard supplies are running dangerously low. When we come to the Carns, you will see how bad things are. We had to dispose of the old Carns weeks ago, while the new ones were barely formed!"

Lief felt Jasmine and Barda's eyes upon him and knew that his companions had at last understood. Grey Guards, made only to serve, made to be cruel, unquestioningly obedient, without a trace of warmth or pity, had only a limited life. When they began to wear out, they were simply thrown away and replaced with identical models.

No wonder this room is forbidden to them, Lief thought. Blindly obedient they might be, but even *they* might react badly if they saw their replacements steadily growing in here.

The white boots turned and began to move back across the room again. The newcomers were inspecting another row of emerging Guards.

Cautiously, Lief, Barda, Jasmine, and Emlis began crawling forward, keeping close to the containers. Moving was a risk, but it was a risk they had to take. If they remained where they were, discovery was certain.

Fortunately, the inspectors were too interested in their work, and their conversation, to notice the tiny, shuffling sounds from the other side of the room.

"These Perns are growing more slowly than the charts predict," the woman commented, as the feet reached the end of the second-last row.

"Well, it is not my fault!" exclaimed her companion. "The power was cut twice yesterday." His voice took on a complaining tone. "It is all the fault of the Conversion Project! It has taken too many materials and far too much of the master's attention of late, in my opinion."

Conversion Project? Lief paused, holding his breath, listening hard. The inspectors had moved forward to the next row and had started pacing slowly back towards the companions' side of the room. It was dangerous to wait, but he had to hear this.

"You seem to have many *opinions*, 3-19," the woman said, her soft voice hardening. "If I were you, I would take care."

"What do you mean?" the man asked peevishly.

"Why do you think the Conversion Project became of first importance to the master, you fool?" snapped the woman, finally losing patience. "It is because the recent disaster in Deltora made him lose faith in the whole idea of Grade 3 Ols. In *you* and your kind, 3-19!"

Lief's heart thudded. The being called 3-19 was a Grade 3 Ol! An example of the most perfect, the most dangerous, of the Shadow Lord's evil shape-changers. Able to mimic humans so perfectly that they could live among them without detection.

Who — or what — was the other speaker then? He burned to see what the two looked like, but did not dare lift his head.

"The master has begun to think that the Grade 3s were a mistake," the woman was continuing. "Too like humans. Prone to pride, curiosity, weakness, and disobedience. And you, 3-19, seem to be proving his point!"

With that, she strode rapidly ahead of her companion. Lief slid forward and ducked hastily out of the side passage just in time to avoid being discovered.

He could see the crouched forms of Barda, Jasmine, and Emlis a few rows ahead of him. He could also see the white-clad legs of the mysterious woman, farther towards the back of the room.

With a thrill of horror, Lief saw that a corner of Emlis's green cloak was trailing into the passage. If the woman looked ahead, looked down . . .

But she seemed to be in no mood to notice her surroundings. One of her feet was tapping impatiently as 3-19 hurried to join her, murmuring apologies and explanations.

". . . did not mean anything by it," Lief heard the Ol say. "I would never question the master's judgment."

"I thought that was exactly what you *were* doing!" snapped the woman, moving into the next row of emerging Grey Guards. "The Conversion Project is the way of the future, 3-19. As you will find out, very soon."

"Soon?" gulped 3-19, thoroughly frightened now. "But I thought — "

"All errors in the process have been corrected," the woman said coldly. "Do you see any fault in *me*?"

There was a moment of stunned silence.

"I — I did not know you were one of them," faltered 3-19 at last.

"Well, I am!" snapped the woman. "Now! Explain to me why these Krops seem thinner than they should be."

They were moving towards the other side of the room once more. Lief, Barda, Jasmine, and Emlis slid out of hiding and began crawling forward as rapidly as they could.

In moments they had drawn almost level with the two inspectors, who by now had almost reached the end of the Krop Pod. Now was the most dangerous time. One by one the companions crossed the gap between containers. They would be in clear view of the two standing at the far end, should either of them turn.

But neither did. Glancing sideways as he scooted from shelter, Lief caught a brief glimpse of two white-clad figures, one tall, one short and slender, standing close together at the end of the container. The short one was consulting a chart. The tall one was bending to turn one of the knobs mounted on the container's shining metal.

Then the figures were out of sight once more as Lief scuttled on after his friends, past the last few pods and across the back wall to the open door.

Keeping low, Jasmine peered cautiously through the doorway. She turned and nodded to the others, then crawled through the opening. Barda and Emlis went after her. But as Lief followed, noting that the room beyond the door was some sort of workroom, he heard the Ol speak again, very timidly.

"The master's plan — "

"The master has many plans!" interrupted the woman sharply. "And none of them are your concern."

Jasmine was beckoning urgently from the other side of the room, but Lief could restrain his curiosity no longer. As soon as he could, he stood up and peered cautiously around the half-open door, back into the pod room.

The two figures had begun their inspection of the next row of Guards. The shorter one, the female,

was consulting the chart. The tall one was walking behind her, glowering.

His thin, sour face was the face of Fallow.

Lief gripped the edge of the door till his knuck-
les turned white. That is not Fallow, he reminded himself desperately. Fallow is dead. That creature, 3-19,
simply wears the same face. But still his breath came
fast and his stomach heaved with loathing.

Then the female figure looked up from the chart
and half turned towards her companion. Bright white
light illuminated her delicate face, her pale blue eyes.

Lief stared for a split second, then shrank back
behind the door, numb with shock.

12 ~ Discoveries

Barda, Jasmine, and Emlis were clustered in front of a narrow door on one side of the workroom. Skirting a long white table cluttered with jars, measuring jugs, and a pot of bubbling green liquid set over a low flame, Lief ran noiselessly to join them.

"There is nowhere to hide in here," Jasmine whispered. "We will have to go farther." She paused as she noticed the expression on Lief's face. "What is it?" she muttered. "You look as if you have seen a ghost."

"I have," Lief whispered back. "That woman — the woman in the pod room — is Tira of Noradz."

Barda and Jasmine gaped at him, horrified.

"Who is Tira?" Emlis asked, looking from one to the other.

"A friend who once risked her life for us," said Jasmine, swallowing hard. "We knew her people had been brought to the Shadowlands. We hoped to find her, to save her. But — "

"But it seems she does not want to be saved." Barda clenched his fists. "She has become the Shadow Lord's creature. What have they done to her?"

"The answer is in there, I think," Jasmine said slowly. She moved aside and pointed to a notice on the door.

CONVERSION
PROJECT
NO ENTRY

There was no sound from behind the door. Lief tried the knob. It turned smoothly. He pushed the door open a crack and peered into the room beyond.

At first, all he could see was a haze of soft pinkish-red light. He blinked, and the room slowly came into focus. It was another, much larger, work-room — huge, silent, and empty. The strange red light glowed from the walls, ceiling, and floor. On the wall facing Lief there were two vast doors, firmly closed.

A wave of dread swept over him. Jasmine was pushing him from behind, urging him on, but for a long moment he resisted her. Everything within him was crying to him to stay where he was. He clutched at the Pirran Pipe beneath his shirt and at last gained enough strength to stumble into the room.

Many work tables jutted from the sidewalls, each one stretching about a third of the way across the room, each one fitted with a set of broad leather straps. Lief's mouth went dry as his imagination suddenly peopled the room. The helpless victims strapped to the benches. The cold, white-clad figures working over them, carrying out their master's orders.

Doing . . . what?

The broad strip of floor in the middle of the room was bare, but scars on its hard surface showed that it had not always been so. Something heavy, large, and square had once stood in the exact center. Shallow ruts, like the tracks of cartwheels, showed that the object had been pulled out of the room by way of the double doors.

There seemed nothing to fear, yet Lief's whole body quivered as he moved towards the marks on the floor. He knew without question that evil itself had been in this red-lit room.

The others felt it, too. Emlis seemed to have shrunk within his cloak, his small face pinched, and his teeth slightly bared. Barda was breathing hard, as though he had been running. Jasmine's face had paled. Filli had disappeared beneath her collar, and Kree was like a black statue on her shoulder.

Instinctively they all avoided stepping on the marks on the floor. They edged past them, pressing against the ends of the work tables, their eyes turned away.

They reached the double doors and, after listening carefully and hearing no sound, ventured through.

A surge of evil power hit them full in their faces, stopping them in their tracks.

They were in a dim, red-lit space with double doors on every wall. The space was completely bare except for a huge, square metal box that stood in the center, where the dented tracks in the floor ended. The box was as tall as Jasmine, and had wheels on its base and a trapdoor at one end. Its hinged lid was open, hanging flat against one of its sides. Clearly, it was the object that had been moved from the workroom.

Evil radiated from it like heat. But the feeling was cold, a deathly cold that seemed to chill their blood, freeze their very bones to ice. Emlis began to whimper.

Lief forced his hand upward and grasped the Pirran Pipe. A little warmth stole through his fingers. He took a step forward.

"Stop!" hissed Jasmine, clutching his arm. "Lief, no! Do not go near it!"

But Lief had to know. He had to see what was inside the box. Clutching the Pipe more tightly he moved forward, Jasmine stumbling behind him, trying to hold him back.

He reached the box and, gritting his teeth, looked over its edge.

At first all he could see was a squirming, pinkish mass. Then his throat closed as he realized what he was looking at — thousands upon thousands of long, pale worms with scarlet heads, thrashing and writhing in a bath of red slime.

And the worms sensed him. They began rearing, trying to reach him, their wicked scarlet heads straining upward, their tails lashing.

With a choking cry Lief jerked backwards, crashing into Barda and Jasmine, who were directly behind him.

He did not need to ask them if they had seen. Their appalled faces told him that they had.

"We have to get out of this place," Barda hissed. He pointed at the double doors to their right. "That way! By my reckoning, the rubbish mounds are on that side. There may be another door . . ."

"No!" Jasmine was shaking her head, pointing to the doors ahead. Barda glared at her, and her pale face flushed scarlet. "We must go on!" she cried desperately. "There must be prisoners here."

Lief looked from one to the other — and at Emlis, cringing behind them.

Jasmine wanted to come here, all along . . .

The thought drifted into his mind, stuck there. He knew it was true.

"Jasmine, who — ?" he began bluntly. He had

just enough time to register Jasmine's startled, guilty expression when a noise from the workroom made him break off.

It was the sound of voices and ringing footsteps. Tira and her companion had finished their inspection far sooner than he had expected.

". . . it cannot be helped!" Tira was exclaiming. "You heard the message. We are needed at once! The Conversion Project is about to be put into action."

The companions glanced around frantically. There was nowhere to hide. Barda grabbed Lief's arm and made for the right-hand doors, with Emlis shuffling after him. After just a moment's hesitation, Jasmine followed.

They swung into chill darkness. The doors had no sooner closed behind them than they heard someone entering the room they had just left.

"Ah, my beauties!" Tira's voice cooed. "Your time has come! I have just had word of it."

There was a creaking sound, then a slam and four clicks as the lid of the box was swung closed and locked into place.

"What is happening?" Jasmine whispered in panic. "What are they going to do with those . . . *things*?"

"Ssss!"

The hiss was startling in the dark silence. Lief, Barda, Jasmine, and Emlis jumped violently and spun around.

Behind them, its roof covered by a tangle of heavy cloth, was an iron cage on wheels. Inside the cage, something moved.

"Help me!" croaked a voice. "Free me, for pity's sake!"

The companions darted silently to the cage. Its door was fastened with a heavy padlock. Peering out through the bars was a gaunt, wild-eyed Dread Gnome, his face just visible in the darkness. "I am Pi-Ban," the gnome gabbled. "Pi-Ban, once of Dread Mountain. Are you the cause of the panic? Did Claw send you? Where are Brianne and Gers?"

Barda grasped two of the cage bars and heaved with all his might. But even his great strength was not enough to bend the thick, rigid iron.

Wordlessly, Jasmine held out her dagger. Lief snatched it and began trying to use its point to open the heavy lock. "Claw did not send us, exactly, Pi-Ban," he whispered. "But we know your name. We know you are one of the people who were taken from the Resistance cave to the east of this place."

"Where are your friends?" Jasmine asked urgently, as Barda began to work on the bars again. "Where are the prisoners kept?"

The gnome groaned, his eyes fixed on Lief's hands. "The dungeons are below ground level," he said, his lips barely moving. "But they are empty now. Moss, Pieter, Tipp, Alexi, Hellena . . . one by one they were taken away. It began the day we were captured, with Moss. It ended yesterday, with Hellena. Only I remain."

"But . . . but surely there are other slaves here?" Jasmine's voice was tense.

"There *were* others, at first," said Pi-Ban. "Many, many others, young and old. Some in the dungeons with us. Some — the quieter, more obedient ones — used to clean and carry. But they, too, are gone now."

"These — these quieter ones," Jasmine said quickly. "Were there any young girls among them?"

"A girl called Tira, for example?" Barda panted, pausing for a moment in his struggle with the cage.

The gnome raised his haggard face. "Is Tira the one you came for?" he asked tiredly. "Yes, I knew her. A gentle creature, with eyes like the sky. She was one of the Noradz — strange, timid folk dressed in black who cleaned the hallways and brought food and water to the dungeons. At first we thought they served the Shadow Lord willingly, but it was not so. They were prisoners, as we were."

Barda nodded grimly and attacked the bars again, as though his enormous hands were tearing at the Shadow Lord himself. Lief was frowning over the lock, lost in concentration.

As if unable to bear watching them any longer, Pi-Ban turned and paced to the back of the cage. He grasped the bars and sank to his knees, staring out into the darkness.

Jasmine edged towards him and kneeled down so that she could talk to him face to face.

"I heard of another girl who might be here, Pi-Ban," she said in a low voice. "Younger than Tira — a child — with black hair and green eyes, called Faith."

She held her breath as Pi-Ban frowned thoughtfully.

"Faith. How strange that you should mention that name," the gnome murmured at last. "I heard it for the first time only a short time ago, when Guards brought me up here. They were Baks, and in worse tempers than usual. Three of their pod had just been slaughtered by a vraal, which was pursuing a fourth into the desert. They had been ordered to abandon him in order to escort me. I told them I was pleased to hear it. That earned me a bruise or two."

A savage white grin shone briefly through the tangles of his matted beard, then he sobered once more. "They told me I was to be taken to the Shadow Arena, and that Faith had gone before me," he muttered. "They seemed to think this would torment me, because I knew this girl. But I do not."

He looked at Jasmine shrewdly. "She is of great importance to *you*, however, that is plain. Who is she, this little girl with black hair and green eyes like your own? And why do you take care to ask of her while your friends cannot hear?"

Her mind whirling, Jasmine turned quickly away from him.

"I cannot do it, Barda!" Lief muttered from the front of the cage. "The lock is too strong. We will have to find another way."

At that moment there was a loud sound from the room they had just left. Doors were being thrown open. There was the pounding of marching feet.

"Guards!" growled Barda.

"Go! Make haste!" Pi-Ban hissed. "There is another pair of doors behind the cage. I think they are a way out."

"No!" Jasmine whispered desperately, standing fast. "We cannot go now!"

"You must!" The gnome raised his tousled head proudly. "If I am to die, I wish to die as a Dread Gnome, not as a coward who drags others down with him. Get out! Save yourselves!"

But already it was too late. The double doors heaved. Dull red light shone through the gap. The Guards were coming through.

13 - The Tunnel

Like lightning, Lief, Barda, and Jasmine leaped for the cage roof, swinging Emlis up behind them. They burrowed under the layers of cloth and lay still, peering out cautiously, their hearts pounding.

"Time to go, scum!" jeered one of the Guards. He approached the cage and jabbed a heavy stick through the bars. There was a shower of sparks, and the companions heard Pi-Ban groan and fall heavily. The Guards bellowed with laughter.

Two white-clad figures strode through the doors — Tira and the Ol called 3-19. The Guards fell abruptly silent.

"You are to go with the cage, 3-19," Tira said crisply. "I will follow with the Project."

"There is only one prisoner," 3-19 objected. "He can walk in chains. The cage is not necessary."

Tira's eyes narrowed. "It is not for you to say what is necessary," she said in a low, dangerous voice. "This prisoner has been kept especially for this moment. We cannot risk escape. He is not to be harmed, so watch the Guards carefully."

3-19 nodded, his thin face sour.

"We Baks do not need an Ol to tell us what to do," mumbled one of the Guards.

"Silence!" Tira shouted. She spun around and returned to the red-lit room where another pod of Guards stood, five on each side of the metal box.

3-19 cleared his throat. "You heard!" he said to the Baks. "Take your positions!"

As the Baks sulkily spaced themselves around the cage, he strode past them and threw open the second set of doors. Faint light flooded into the room, bringing with it the foul smell of the mounds.

Lief lay rigid, fearing that at any moment they would be seen, but there was no cry of alert. The Guards were staring resentfully at 3-19, whose eyes were fixed on the way ahead.

"Forward!" shouted Tira from the other room.

"Move!" 3-19 muttered to the Baks.

"We must pull down the covers first," one growled.

With a sickening thud, Lief realized that the pieces of cloth beneath which he and his companions were hiding were flaps designed to be pulled down over the sides of the cage.

"There is no need for the covers, you fool!" snapped 3–19. "It is night! The prisoners will see nothing."

"A travelling cage must be covered," the Guard said stubbornly. "Those are the orders. We Baks always . . ."

"You Baks are overdue for the scrap heap, and the sooner you are there the better!" spat 3-19 in fury. "Move!"

Muttering darkly, the six Baks put their shoulders to the cage and heaved it into the foul-smelling night. Behind them rumbled the great metal box.

Pi-Ban lay dazed and mumbling. Lief, Barda, Jasmine, and Emlis were clinging desperately to the lurching cage roof. Each of the Shadow Lord servants was occupied with his or her own thoughts of resentment or triumph.

And so it was that no one saw three shadows creep from the shelter of the mounds and follow.

✳

At first, all Lief could hear was the rattling of the cage, but after a while he began to pick up voices from below.

"We deserve more respect," a Guard was grumbling. "We gave the alert! *We* were the ones outside, fighting the vraal. *We* were the ones who heard those wrecks on the scrap heap calling."

Lief felt his scalp prickle. He listened intently.

"The Ol said we should be on the scrap heap ourselves, Bak 3," another Guard said.

"The Ol is a fool!" snarled Bak 3. "You *know* we don't have a fail date like other pods, Bak 9. We were told that from the first, and warned not to boast of it to the others. Have you forgotten?"

"No," Bak 9 mumbled. "But the Ol said — "

"Forget what it said!" Bak 3 snapped. "The master would never dispose of us! Why, *we* gave him the news he was waiting for — the news of the girl and the black bird. Why else are we going to the Arena now?"

Lief's heart thudded violently. The Shadow Lord had been waiting for Jasmine. He had been expecting her. It was news of *her* that had caused this haste.

The suspicion Lief had been fighting ever since they arrived in the Shadowlands reared its head once more and this time he faced it squarely. Jasmine had a secret — a dangerous secret. She had led them to the Factory. She had refused to escape, when escape was still possible.

He burned to turn his head, to whisper to Jasmine, ask her to explain. But he did not dare. The slightest sound or movement might betray them.

Through a gap in the cloth he could see that the cage was rounding the hill he had seen from the Factory. The Guards panted as they hauled the grating wheels into the curve.

Then, all at once, the road had straightened again. Now it was running right beside the mountains. Ahead was a vast, lighted Arena. There was the sound of a great, murmuring crowd.

"Faster!" shouted Tira from behind, her voice sharp with excitement. "Stop in the tunnel, 3-19! The Project is to go into the Arena first. Do you hear me?"

"I am not deaf!" barked 3-19. "Guards! More speed!"

"We are not deaf either, Ol," growled Bak 9.

The cage began to move faster. The noise of the crowd grew louder. Then suddenly the light dimmed, and the cage creaked to a halt. Lief saw dark stone and guessed that they were in the entrance tunnel that led through the walls of the Arena.

He felt a wave of sickness, heard the sound of heavy wheels, and realized that the metal box was being moved past the cage so that it could enter the Arena first.

"Wait here until you are summoned, 3-19!" Tira's voice echoed from somewhere ahead.

"Is the woman in red the slave Faith?" 3-19 asked curiously.

Lief felt Jasmine tense.

"Of course not!" Tira snapped. "She is the way of the future, as I am. The slave is chained below the platform. Perns! Forward!"

A drum began to beat — a deep, throbbing sound like a great heartbeat. The crowd fell silent.

Lief had to see what was happening. Cautiously he tweaked a little more of the cover aside.

The metal box, with Tira walking before it, was being pushed through a vast archway not far ahead. It was moving from darkness into blazing light. The light of the Arena.

Lief knew that there must be tiers of seats circling the Arena, but he could not see them from where he was lying. Neither could he see the vraals, whose growls were mingling with the beating of the great drum. But he could see the ground clearly. Everything within the frame of the arch was as clear as day. It was like looking at a vast, moving picture.

Grey Guards holding sparking rods lined the path along which the metal box was passing. The path led to a huge platform ringed with white columns. Someone wearing a long red robe was standing there, too far back for Lief to see clearly.

Behind the Guards were ragged people, pressed closely together. The peoples' shoulders were bowed, their eyes haunted and despairing. Most bore the Shadow Lord's brand on brow or cheek. They stood dully watching as Tira and the metal box passed them by.

Lief's eyes burned as he saw among them the black-clad people of Noradz, the hulking figures of hundreds of Jalis, some palace guards. Others he did not recognize. But he knew who they were. Farmers from the northeast, the west, and the Plains, gladiators from Rithmere, fishing folk from the coast, Resistance fighters, citizens of Del . . .

Deltorans, all of them. Beaten, worked, and swept by the wind of despair until they had no heart or hope left. They believed they had been brought here to die. For many, perhaps, death might seem a relief from the misery of their slavery.

But they will not die, Lief thought grimly. And they will be slaves no longer. They will not!

But there were so many. Uneasily Lief fingered the Pirran Pipe beneath his shirt. The Pipe's moment of testing was near. Would its magic give them time to rally the people? To get so many thousands out of the Arena? Would it break the shutting spell blocking the mountains?

The box had nearly reached the platform. And the light in the Arena was changing to a dull, angry red.

Dawn.

A movement caught Lief's eye. The Baks were stealing closer to the archway. 3-19 was looking resentfully after Tira. No one was watching the cage.

"This is our chance to get down!" Barda muttered.

"No!" Jasmine whispered urgently. "We must stay here. How else are we to reach the platform safely?"

"The platform?" exclaimed Barda, aghast. "Why — "

Lief was sure that Jasmine had her own reasons

for wanting to get to the platform. But he, too, believed that the center of the Arena was where they should be.

"The Pipe must be played where the Shadow Lord can hear it clearly," he whispered. "And the people must see us. Emlis, as soon as we reach the platform, I will pass the Pipe to you. Be ready!"

Emlis squeaked frightened agreement.

"This is a reckless plan, Lief," Barda growled. "The people have had no warning. They will not know — "

"Shh!" breathed Jasmine.

Lief froze. Then he heard what Jasmine had heard before him. At the back of the cage there were tiny noises. Whispering voices. A clink as someone lifted the cage lock. A grunt of effort and a muttered curse.

Then something tapped Lief's foot.

"Get down, you fools!" rasped a harsh voice. "We cannot release Pi-Ban, but you at least we can save."

Claw!

"No. We are staying with the cage," Lief whispered.

"Are you mad, boy?" Claw hissed.

"There is no time to explain," said Barda rapidly. "If you wish to help us, get into the Arena. Tell the people — as many as you can — to be ready to fight their way out. When it is time, they will know it."

"If we try to save them all, they will be slaughtered," rasped Claw. "And we with them. A few we might — "

"Tell them to make for the pass behind the Arena!" Barda broke in. "Now move away, Claw, for pity's sake. The Guards will turn and see you!"

"The pass is sealed by the shutting spell," Claw said.

"Leave that to us," said Barda. "Just tell them!"

"You are mad!" muttered Claw. The talon resting on Lief's foot tightened briefly, then slipped away.

They heard more whispering. Then silence. Claw, Brianne, and Gers had vanished into the shadows.

"Will he do it?" Jasmine murmured.

"Who can say?" said Barda grimly. "And I fear we are as mad as he claims! For all we know, the Pirran Pipe will trouble the Shadow Lord no more than a buzzing fly."

"Look!" Jasmine whispered.

A red-clad woman was walking forward on the platform, her strong face and smooth silver hair now clearly visible.

"Hellena!"

The despairing, unbelieving cry had come from below them. From Pi-Ban.

3-19 swung around. "Return to your posts!" he spat at the Guards furiously, then turned back to the Arena.

The red-robed woman had also heard Pi-Ban's cry. Her lips curved in a cool smile.

Lief stared, horrified. Hellena had been a member of Pi-Ban's group. She was the friend for whom Brianne had mourned so bitterly. Yet now her eyes gleamed in triumph as the Perns slid the metal box up a ramp and onto the platform. She was revelling in evil. Like Tira.

The Conversion Project . . . the way of the future . . .

"There will be no vraals released today," Hellena cried in ringing tones.

Howls of disappointment rose from the audience — howls that changed abruptly to wails as thunder cracked and a ghastly chill swept through the Arena.

The Baks cringed beside the cage. "The master is present," Bak 3 whimpered.

"Today a new era begins!" Hellena cried. "After today, nothing will stand in the master's way. Wherever he lays his hand, all will bow down before him and do his will. As you will see."

She raised her hand. "Bring Faith!"

Two Guards came up to the platform dragging between them a small, struggling, black-haired girl whose green eyes flashed fury.

Jasmine caught her breath.

Lief's heart seemed to stop. Barda cursed softly.

The child on the platform, her small face so like Jasmine's that the two could only be sisters, was scanning the crowd, her eyes filled with fearful hope.

"This is the sister of one of the master's most vicious enemies!" shouted Hellena. "But, like the gnome who will be joining her — a gnome I know to be the worst of traitors — she will soon bow willingly before the master."

The audience roared.

"We are about to be summoned," gabbled Bak 9 fearfully. "The master will think we have disobeyed our orders. Dawn has broken, and the cage is uncovered."

Lief tensed, the child Faith suddenly the last thing on his mind. Surely disaster would not strike now, when they were so close!

The other Baks shuffled their feet nervously. "The Ol said — " one began.

"Curse the Ol!" snarled Bak 9. And without further warning the six sprang up onto the sides of the cage and ripped the covers aside.

Emlis, suddenly exposed, rolled in an agony of terror and fell. He hit the ground and lay still. Lief, Barda, and Jasmine struggled to rise, to draw their weapons, but they had no chance. The Guards recovered from their shock in an instant. The sparking rods thrashed down, down . . .

Lief saw Jasmine crumple and fall back, Kree with her. He saw Barda hit once, twice. Then he himself felt a fiery jolt on the back of his neck. Agony shot through him. Then all was darkness.

14 ~ The Shadow Arena

Lief came to his senses slowly. Something was thumping, thumping, every thunderous beat sending shooting pain through his head. He was lying on a hard, jolting surface that was jarring his aching bones . . .

He forced his eyes open. His head was jammed against cold bars. He could see nothing beyond the bars, because thick fabric hung over them on the outside.

It took some time to remember what had happened and then to realize, with cold horror, where he was. He was in the cage, and it was moving through the Arena. The sound he could hear was the beating of the great drum.

Barda and Jasmine were stirring beside him. Pi-Ban was crouched by Barda's head, his face the picture of despair.

Lief felt for his sword, but of course it was gone. With a thrill of terror he moved his hand to his neck, and relief rushed through him as he felt the cord unbroken and the Pirran Pipe still hanging beneath his shirt.

Rough voices were muttering somewhere near. Lief realized that they were the voices of the Guards who were pushing the cage on his side.

"The Ol will try to claim the credit."

"Let it try! When the covers come off, its face will show its surprise. The master will understand that it was the Baks who brought him the three, and that the Ol knew nothing of it."

"That scrawny Wild One that was with them — "

Emlis! thought Lief, looking wildly around the cage. Then he remembered. The last he had seen of Emlis was when the little Keron fell from the cage in the tunnel.

Another Guard was speaking. Lief closed his eyes, straining to hear. As he listened, his heart sank.

"The Wild One was damaged. It crawled away to die. Forget it. It is the three the master wants. Boy. Big man. Girl with black bird. We had fine luck, Bak 3."

"And what a fool the Ol will look!"

Low, sly guffaws.

Wincing at the pain in his head, Lief hauled himself to the front of the cage. At the corner, the cover flaps gaped apart. He squinted through the gap.

Ahead, the Ol, 3-19, stalked straight-backed towards the platform where Tira waited, her face like thunder. Beside Tira stood Hellena, one hand holding Faith's chain, the other resting on the lid of the metal box.

Behind the Grey Guards lining the path pressed the mass of dull-eyed, ragged people. And beyond, rising out of sight, were tiers of seats crowded with onlookers — onlookers of every shape, color, and size.

The audience seemed to be shimmering, shifting, wavering . . . Lief rubbed his eyes.

Then he realized that his eyes were not at fault. There were a few Ra-Kacharz on the benches, some pods of Guards, and a rabble of Wild Ones. But most of the audience were Ols — Grade 1 and 2 Ols, whose shapes kept changing, melting, and re-forming as he watched.

Here, of course, there was no need to deceive. The lower-grade Ols did not have to hold one shape if they did not wish it. They could change at will, for their own entertainment or use.

He focused on one pair as their horned, goat-like heads dissolved into gaping fish-faces, their hands became fins, their color changed from brown to silver-green, their bodies swelled. This crowded the pair beside them, two women in red bonnets. The women hissed angrily, and for an instant showed their true shape — white and formless, with gaping toothless mouths and eyes like coals. The next moment the white shapes shrank and narrowed, becoming writhing snakes with human faces.

Sickened, Lief looked down again. At the slaves, standing so still and so silent.

And then — then he saw something strange. No one appeared to be moving, but it was as though ripples were passing through the crowd.

He pressed his face against the bars. Yes! The same tiny actions were being repeated by one person after another. A small turn of the head. Lips moving, so slightly that it would be impossible to see from a distance that words were being said.

A message was being passed among the slaves. And Lief was sure he knew where the message had begun. With Claw, Brianne, and Gers, mingling with the crowd at the edge of the Arena. Whispering the same words over and over again.

Watch the platform. Be ready to fight. Get to the road behind the Arena. Pass it on.

"The word is spreading," said Barda's voice in his ear. "We must stop it!"

Lief turned. Barda was behind him, looking over his head into the Arena. The big man's eyes were deeply shadowed. A great red burn marked his brow where a sparking rod had struck him.

"It is too late to stop it now," Lief said.

"But everything has changed, and plainly Claw, Brianne, and Gers do not know it!" Barda whispered urgently. "They must have been hiding outside the tunnel when we were captured, and saw nothing. If they can see the cage covered now, they no doubt think it is all part of the plan."

Lief felt for the Pirran Pipe and slipped it from its casing. Tingling warmth flowed through his fingers, and a strange peace stole over him. "Nothing has changed, Barda," he said calmly. "You cannot cage a sound. When we reach the platform, I will play the Pipe exactly as planned. Not as Emlis might have done, but as well as I can."

"Whatever else the Pipe may do, it will not melt iron bars, Lief," said Barda grimly. "The others may escape. But we will be trapped."

Then so it will have to be, Lief thought. Claw, Brianne, and Gers can lead the people to freedom as well as we can. But he said nothing.

Looking around for Jasmine, he saw that she had also woken and crawled to the front of the cage. But she had not come to join her companions. She was crouched in the other corner, peering through the gap in the covers there.

Trying to catch a glimpse of Faith, Lief thought. The sister she has been seeking all along.

He moved to Jasmine's side, touched her hand. "Jasmine," he whispered. "Why did you not tell me of Faith?"

Jasmine turned on him, her eyes dark with misery. "Tell *you*? How can you ask that?" she said in a low voice.

Lief stared at her, aghast. "What — what do you mean?" he stammered.

Jasmine clenched her fists. "Do you still try to deceive me, Lief, even now?" she hissed. "Do you not understand? I *know*. I know what you did!"

"What?" Lief asked wildly.

The word was no sooner out of his mouth when the cage's front wheels hit the foot of the ramp with a thump. He, Barda, and Jasmine were thrown violently backwards. The Pirran Pipe flew out of Lief's hand and began to roll towards the back of the cage. He snatched for it frantically and managed to catch it just as the Guards, grunting with effort, tilted the cage and began to haul it upward. Another second and the Pipe would have slipped through the bars and been lost.

His heart beating fast at the near disaster, Lief crawled back to the front of the cage.

Forget everything, he told himself. Everything except what must be done. He felt a familiar dread chill and knew that the cage was nearing the metal box. He gripped the Pirran Pipe more tightly.

"Attention, slaves!" Hellena cried. "I have something of importance to tell you! Listen well!"

Lief reached the cage corner and peered through the gap. Tira was standing right beside it, with 3-19.

"Why is the cage covered?" Tira muttered furiously to 3-19, glancing nervously upward.

"The Baks did it," said 3-19 sullenly. "By the

time I saw their disobedience, the summons had come and it was too late to take the covers off."

"You are an incompetent fool!" Tira spat. "How glad I am that the master has finished with you and your kind."

She turned away and 3-19 glared at her, his long fingers twitching as though he longed to fasten them around her slender neck.

Tira had moved to stand beside Hellena. Hellena raised her arms.

"Once I was a deadly enemy of the master," Hellena cried. "I freed his slaves. I killed his servants. I confess it. And my companion was once the foulest of rebels — a creeping, deceitful spy who secretly helped the master's foes!"

Tira lifted her chin. "I confess it!" she said loudly.

Lief heard Barda's soft groan behind him, but did not look around.

Hellena's cold, glittering gaze swept over the Arena. "Now, we are both free of doubt, fear, and evil thoughts. Thanks to the gift the master has bestowed on us, we are not only his servants, but his eyes and ears as well."

Lovingly, her hand smoothed the metal box. "Like us, you deserve death, slaves. But the master is merciful. You are all to share his gift. Soon your struggles will be at an end. You will belong to the master, as we do."

The audience cheered wildly. The slaves on the floor of the Arena were deathly still. Hellena smiled coldly.

"There is no need to fear, slaves, whatever rumors you may have heard," she said. "The Conversion process has been perfected. It is safe, efficient, and simple. Once released, the carriers of the master's gift will find their own way to you. They are slim and very fast. The process will take no time at all."

She touched her ear. "A brief moment's pain — here — and the master will be with you always. Your Conversion will bring you freedom. You will return to your homes, mingle with your people, and do the master's will gladly."

Lief's skin was crawling. At last he understood what had happened to Tira and Hellena. He understood what the hideous worms were — what they did. He saw the Shadow Lord's plan.

The master has many plans . . .

Into Lief's mind sprang a terrifying picture. Thousands of prisoners set free by the Shadow Lord, returning to Deltora, received with joy and welcome. Thousands of prisoners who looked and sounded exactly as they had before, but who carried the Enemy within their brains, guiding their every thought, their every deed.

Thousands of prisoners, in whose keeping, safe in bags or pockets, were more of the deadly scarlet-headed worms. So that at night, while their families and neighbors slept . . .

Hellena had begun speaking again. "Though there is no escape from the master's gift, it is best if you do not struggle," she said. "With the help of the slave Faith and the gnome who once fought side by side with me against the master, I will show you how easy it can be."

She turned to the Guards. "Remove the covers!" she ordered.

15 - The Trap

The covers were swept from the cage. Light streamed in, mercilessly exposing the four people who had sprung to their feet and backed against the bars. Lief heard 3-19 shouting in anger and the Baks' loud, triumphant explanations. He saw Tira and Hellena looking up with shining eyes at the red smoke swirling in the tower above them, and the dark shadow within it.

Lightning cracked the boiling clouds. A thunderous gale crashed downward, throwing Lief and the others off their feet, pinning them down. The cage shuddered, its wheels bent by the force of the blast.

Gasping for breath, unable to move, pressed down, down by the howling wind, Lief heard the screams of the slaves writhing helplessly in the Arena, the cries of Tira and Hellena, the grunts of the Baks and the Perns on the platform as they struggled to rise.

Screeching, the seven Ak-Baba swooped downward, riding the gale, talons outstretched, hooked beaks gaping. The columns that ringed the platform trembled and came to life. Ols! Hissing white flames with darkness at their hearts, with gaping, toothless mouths, hollow eyes, and clutching hands, they rose and stood against the force of the wind. And with a grating crash, stone doors slid into place, sealing the Arena.

Then Lief knew that not only Jasmine but *all* of them had been expected. The Enemy had not known how, or where, they would appear. But he had known they would come. He had prepared for it.

There was one thing, though, that the Enemy had not expected. Eyes watering, almost deafened by the roaring wind, Lief began dragging the Pirran Pipe towards his lips. Slowly, slowly he forced his hand upward.

"3-19! The prisoners are down! They are ready!" Tira shrieked against the gale. "Open the Conversion Project!"

The Ol in the shape of Fallow walked to the metal box, moving easily, untroubled by the wind. He put his hand to the catch that fastened the trapdoor.

"3-19!" Lief shouted with all his strength. "Beware!"

The Ol turned its head to look at him blankly.

"Do not listen!" screamed Tira. "3-19! I order you!"

"You will be finished if you open that box, Ol!" Lief shouted. "With humans to do his will, your master will have no need of you. You and all your kind will lie rotting in the scrap mounds with the Guards."

3-19 hesitated, frowning.

"Baks! Perns!" cried Tira in fury.

But the Baks and Perns, scrabbling on the boards of the platform, could not move, any more than she could.

Lief's hand, clutching the Pipe, had reached his chest. He forced it on towards his mouth. He needed one more moment. One more . . .

Red smoke rushed from the tower, ferocious malice at its heart. Eyes blazed within the smoke. Shadowy hands reached out.

3-19 cried out in agony, crumpled, and fell. The trapdoor at the end of the box burst open. Scarlet-headed worms streamed out in a great flood, spreading, greedily seeking, into the cage.

Lief could feel them seething over his feet, his legs. Jasmine and Barda's panic-stricken cries were ringing in his ears. Kree was screeching despairingly. Pi-Ban gave a single, high scream. Lief screwed his eyes shut, concentrating all his strength on a final, desperate effort.

Then he had the Pipe to his lips. He blew. One pure, clear note.

The piercing sound rose and echoed around the

walls of the Arena, and on to the mountains beyond.

And with the sound, the stream of worms halted. The worms thrashed, twisting and dying like leeches of the Forbidden Way exposed to the light.

The red smoke recoiled in a clap of thunder that shook the ground. The gale died, and the Ak-Baba lurched in the skies. The Ols lowered their grasping hands and stood, swaying. The beings on the tiers of seats bent and groaned. The vraals howled in their cages.

The slaves in the Arena had been told to wait for the signal. What more of a signal did they need? They leaped to their feet and surged forward in a great wave. The confused Guards lining the pathway stumbled and fell, crushed beneath their weight.

But there was no way out. No way out of the Arena, sealed with doors of stone. No way to reach the pass to freedom. Nowhere to run. Nowhere to hide.

Gasping, staggering to his feet, Lief drew breath. The red smoke swelled and twisted above him, the shadow within it gathering strength. Again he blew, and again the piercing note echoed through the Arena, thunder cracked, and the smoke recoiled.

Lief saw Pi-Ban rising, wide-eyed, a shrivelled worm falling from his ear and onto his shoulder. He saw Barda and Jasmine hauling themselves up, clinging to the cage bars.

Outside the cage, the guards milled, confused. Tira and Hellena had fallen to their knees, staring with dazed disgust at the worms that had dropped away from them onto the platform. Faith stood alone, pale as a ghost.

"Faith!" shrieked Jasmine. "Get the keys to the cage!"

The child turned and looked, unsmiling. Her lips opened. Then came the voice — a low, deadly whisper that chilled the blood.

"There is no escape, Jasmine."

Jasmine stared, frozen. The voice whispered on.

"From the moment you looked into the crystal, from the moment you let me into your mind, you were doomed. I knew you would come to me. I had only to wait. But do not think I cared about you. You were only bait. I knew that wherever you went, *he* would follow."

Then the girl laughed, horribly. And laughing she shimmered, faded, and disappeared in a drift of red smoke, like the phantom she was.

Jasmine screamed and screamed again, clutching the cage bars in shock, grief, and horror. Shock that what she had thought flesh and blood had been a mirage. Grief for a child who had never existed. Horror as she realized how cunningly, how completely, she had been deceived.

Into Lief's mind flashed a memory. Tirral, speaking on the Isle of Keras.

There are many ways to catch a fish. And if the fish you want rises to a simple bait, so much the better.

Jasmine rose to the Shadow Lord's bait, and so did I in turn, Lief thought. How easy it all was! How easily he lured us into this trap. Using our weaknesses. Jasmine's loneliness and impatience. My love for Jasmine.

"For the Jalis!" The words roared amid the thunder. Then Gers was leaping onto the platform — Gers, leading a ragged army of his tribe. Some of the Jalis flung themselves, roaring, on the panicking Baks and Perns. Others set their great hands on two of the cage bars and heaved.

The iron bent like butter. Pi-Ban scrambled through the gap. Barda followed, half-carrying Jasmine. Then came Lief, the Pipe still pressed to his lips.

Again Lief had to draw breath. Again the red smoke writhed and lunged. Again it drew back as the Pipe sounded once more.

But the Enemy was gaining strength. Each time the Pipe repelled him, he drew back a little less. The seven Ak-Baba hovered around him, their unearthly cries mingling with the thunder. Within the smoke's core, malicious eyes were gleaming.

How long could the Pipe hold the shadows back?

And then, Lief heard it. Through the sound of the Pipe, through the rumbling of the thunder, came a faint, exhausted wail.

Lief swung around. But Jasmine had heard the sound, too. Jasmine and Barda had gone back to the cage. They were kneeling beside it, peering under its base, shouting to Gers.

Then the Jalis and Barda were heaving at the cage, tilting it while Jasmine slid underneath and emerged dragging a small figure in a green, hooded cape. Emlis!

Lief could not speak. Could do nothing but go on playing the Pipe. But he watched and listened as Emlis staggered to his feet.

Emlis was babbling of crawling under the cage in the tunnel, of clinging to the cage's underside as it was rolled to the platform. He was telling of being trapped when the cage's wheels bent beneath the force of the wind. Of being pinned, helpless, unable to scramble free, unable to make anyone hear him, until now . . .

Then Emlis was beside Lief, taking the Pipe from Lief's hand. Emlis was playing. And for the first time in countless centuries, the land that had once been Pirra heard the true song of the Pirran Pipe.

For as Ak-Baba shrieked and the red smoke shrank back into the boiling sky, as the Ols crouched, moaning, and the prisoners listened in awe, Emlis played like the Pipers of old. Emlis played on the Pirran Pipe the music of his own heart.

The exquisite sound filled the Arena, echoed from the mountains, rang on the Factory walls, and rolled on over the parched plain. In it was mourning for ancient beauties lost, anger at evil that seeks only to rule and destroy, fear for what might be. And then, a deep longing for home.

Not Pirra, despoiled, transformed, and gone forever. But the only home Emlis knew.

A home where deep waters rippled and soft sands drifted on peaceful shores. A place where the light was soft and cool, and the gentle, lapping sound of water filled the air. A place missed, and ached for.

Lief stood, transfixed. His heart seemed to be breaking as the music rose, pleading for rescue, crying for release.

Then . . . the Arena disappeared.

Cold, freezing cold. Rushing darkness . . .

And the next instant Lief was struggling in black, icy water, the panicking cries of thousands ringing in his ears.

What had happened? What new sorcery was this?

"Jasmine!" he screamed.

"Here!" Barda bobbed up beside him, supporting Jasmine and Pi-Ban. Lief took Jasmine from him, held her head above the water, felt the rush of Kree's wings.

"My music!" Emlis swam like an eel towards them. "My people heard it! They brought us home! The Shadow Lord will never know what became of us!"

"*Our* people will drown, Emlis!" choked Jasmine. "Oh, there are so many! Far too many for the Kerons to save in time. They will drown!"

Then Lief heard her gasp, and the next moment light flooded the darkness, pushing it back, back, as the magical music of the Pirran Pipe had made the Enemy shrink and retreat. And with the light came a rushing, rippling sound. Lief pulled himself around, shivering. He blinked, hardly able to believe his eyes.

For coming towards them was a vast fleet of boats. The shell-like craft of the Plumes, the elegant new boats of the Aurons, the heavy longboats of the Kerons, paddling together, scooping struggling people from the water, hauling them to safety.

Clef and Azan paddled furiously to keep up with Auron guards on twisting eels and stolid Keron leech-gatherers. Nols, Piper of the Plumes, rowed beside Tirral, Piper of the Kerons, as Tirral searched the black waters for her son, whose music had summoned them all.

But it was Penn, the Auron history-keeper, who lifted Lief and his companions from the water. And it was with her that they began their long journey home.

16 ~ Reunions

The people slept as they were carried through the caverns. Only Pi-Ban was woken, to wring the hands of Lief, Barda, and Jasmine, and then to be spirited up to Dread Mountain, above the emerald sea.

"I fear he will tell of his adventures, whatever my warnings," Lief murmured. "The Dread Gnomes are great storytellers, Penn."

"Pi-Ban will not tell," Penn said serenely. "He will forget with his first breath of the air above. Do you not know, Lief? You have read Doran's rhyme."

Lief bent his head, remembering. " 'Where timeless tides swamp memory . . .' " he murmured at last.

"Yes. The seas of the underground are the seas of forgetting," Penn smiled. "How do you think we have lived here in secret so long?"

"But in the Shadowlands we remembered," Barda objected.

"You had Emlis with you," said Penn. "And the minds of all of us were focused on you, besides."

"But when we return home, we will forget?" asked Jasmine, very grave.

Penn smiled, and took from her pocket three small, smooth stones. "Not if you keep these with you," she said, handing one stone to each companion. "They are soul-stones. All Aurons carry one. Doran carried his always, so it is said. And these are yours."

Lief, Barda, and Jasmine looked down at the stones. They seemed to change hue every moment — gleaming gold, red, green, blue, black, purple, and all the colors of the rainbow in turn.

"I cannot tell the real color," Barda said in wonder.

"That is because there is none," Penn said simply. "It is the eye of the observer that makes the difference. And so it is with people, we found, when the Pipe sang in our caverns for the first time, not long ago."

"That is how . . . ?" Jasmine began.

Penn nodded. "We on Auron heard the Pipe. Its song made us remember that once our people were one. We set out to see for ourselves, at last, the others of our kind, and to find out what had happened to you. At the Forbidden Way we met the Plumes, who had travelled north for the same reason. They did not seem as savage as we had feared. And so together we called to the Kerons, bidding them to light the tunnel and allow us entry to their territory."

"And Tirral agreed?" asked Barda disbelievingly.

Penn smiled. "After a time," she said placidly. "It seems that, like us, she and her people had been giving thought to the wisdom of keeping up old rivalries in times of trouble. We learned that her son had gone with you to the Shadowlands. Then, together, we all waited for the sound that would tell us that he, and you — and the Pipe — were ready to return. Together, at last, we heard it, and together we brought you back."

"Without you we would have perished," said Lief. "We owe you our lives."

"Without you, the Pirrans would have remained apart forever," Penn answered. "We owe you even more."

✳

The Pirran fleet skimmed through the caverns like leaves blown by the wind. There was much time for talk and for reunion, however, for many boats paddled for a time beside Penn's own. Clef and Azan came, their craft riding low in the water under the sleeping weight of Claw, Brianne, and Gers. Nols came, Tira and Hellena peaceful at her feet. And Tirral came with Emlis, who had thrown off his leech-gatherer's cloak with relief.

"My son seems taller than when he went away," Tirral said.

"He has grown in more than stature," Barda answered. "He has a great heart."

"When I am a little older — old enough to wear a leech-gatherer's cloak in comfort — I am going to be an explorer like Doran," Emlis said shyly. "I will explore and map the caverns. I will travel the seas of the Plumes and the Aurons, and unknown seas as well."

"Seas of soft purple," murmured Lief. "Black seas filled with stars. Caverns that glitter like diamonds."

"How do you know?" Emlis asked in surprise.

But Tirral put her hand inside her cloak and brought out something that gleamed in the magic light. She passed it to Lief. He stared down at it, almost as if he had forgotten what it was.

"I return the Belt of Deltora to you," Tirral said formally. "In exchange for the Pirran Pipe."

"Thank you." Lief hesitated. There was more he wished to say, but he decided it would not be wise. Very aware of Barda's and Jasmine's eyes upon him, he fastened the gleaming thing about his waist, and kept silent.

✳

At last, in the golden cavern of the topaz, it was time to say farewell.

"We have brought you to the place where the signs of life above are strongest," Penn said to the companions softly, as the fleet gathered around them. "From here, all your people can travel home."

"Lief! Barda! Jasmine!"

Lief turned and saw Emlis waving to them, not far off. He was still holding the Pirran Pipe.

The companions waved back. "And what of the Pipe, Penn?" Lief asked. "Will it be separated into three parts once more?"

"No," said Penn. "The Kerons will keep it for now. It was decided, before you returned, that if it should ever come back to us, it would remain complete. It will stay with each tribe for one full year, to be played morning, noon, and evening by the Piper as is the Pirran way. Then it will be passed on, in a great festival organized by the tribe who is giving it up."

Her eyes twinkled. "I daresay there will be much competition," she added. "The tribes will try to outdo one another, and every festival will be greater and more exciting than the last. But I, at least, will not complain. Festivals are far better than war. And no one enjoys a feast better than I do. Well — are you ready?"

Lief swallowed and nodded. "Farewell, Penn," he said. He took Barda's and Jasmine's hands in his own and closed his eyes.

"Farewell," he heard Penn whisper. And the now familiar darkness closed in around them.

✳

They opened their eyes on the light of Deltora. It was just past dawn. The grass on which they lay was still wet with dew. The sky was palest blue, faintly streaked with pink. A breeze stirred the trees and brushed their faces, fresh and sweet.

Lief felt he had never seen such beauty.

He saw that they were in the gardens of the palace, near the stairs to the great entrance hall. Two palace guards were standing at the doors.

For an instant the guards stared, astounded, at the crowd that had appeared on the palace lawn from thin air. Then they turned and raced inside, shouting the news at the tops of their voices.

Jasmine raised her face to the sun. Kree took flight, stretching his injured wing, screeching joyously. Barda gave a great sigh.

All around them people were opening their eyes, sitting up, staring in unbelieving joy. In the blink of an eye, it seemed to them, they had been swept from the Shadow Arena to this beautiful place that looked and smelled like home. Most were convinced that they were dreaming.

But there, slowly climbing to their feet, were the three strangers who had stood on the Arena platform before them. One was the boy who had played the strange Pipe. Around his waist he wore something that glittered and shone. A belt of steel, studded with seven great gems.

The slaves who were no longer slaves stared in wonder, gradually accepting the truth.

Deltora had not abandoned them. They had

never been forgotten. They were free. And it was their king who had brought them home.

The doors of the palace flew open. People began to stream down the stairs, many still heavy-eyed with sleep but all shouting and opening their arms. The people on the grass stood up and stumbled to meet them. The two crowds met and mingled, loved ones and strangers alike embracing, weeping, and laughing for joy.

The palace bells began to ring, calling to the people of the city below. Jasmine touched Lief's arm. He looked down at her, his heart very full. She murmured something, but he could not hear her over the noise of the bells. He bent closer.

"I said, it is shame to me that I ever doubted you, Lief," Jasmine repeated awkwardly. "But Faith seemed so real. And she said — "

"The fault is mine," Lief said quickly. "I was a fool to refuse to speak of the crystal, to pretend it did not exist. I did tell you and Barda of it once, after I saw it in a dream in the Valley of the Lost. I thought you would remember."

Jasmine looked puzzled. "I think I did, at first," she said slowly. "But then I looked in the crystal, and forgot everything but the lie I saw there." She looked down. "I should have known that you would never deceive me."

Lief hesitated. This was the moment he had been

dreading. He glanced at Barda, who was stolidly pretending not to listen. He cleared his throat. "I *have* deceived you, Jasmine," he said loudly. "You, and Barda too. There is something — "

He broke off. Jasmine's hand had slipped from his arm. She was looking towards the palace.

A small group of people had appeared at the doors, looking eagerly out into the crowd. Sharn and Doom stood to one side, supporting Josef between them. On the other side was Stephen the pedlar, beaming, arm in arm with a strange, tall woman whose shaved head was painted with swirling designs. But in the center stood Ranesh, his face expressionless, Zeean of Tora, and a graceful figure wrapped in a long cloak.

Marilen.

17 ~ Secrets

His heart in his mouth, Lief took a step forward. Marilen saw him. With a final glance at Ranesh, she gathered up her cloak and walked slowly down the stairs, her head held high. Lief felt Jasmine and Barda drawing back from him as she approached.

The celebrating crowd seethed around them, but the four — the three companions and the approaching girl — had eyes and ears only for one another. It was as though they were on an island in time and space.

Her face glowing with relief and welcome, Marilen held out her hands. Lief took them.

"Oh, Lief, how I have longed for your return!" Marilen murmured. "How I wished I could tell you . . . all is well, Lief! All is well. We are safe."

Lief bowed his head, overwhelmed by thankfulness. He felt the girl's hands move away from his.

He glanced behind him. Barda was looking straight ahead, but Jasmine met his eyes with a determined smile.

Lief had a moment of confusion. Could it be that his companions already knew the secret he had kept from them so long?

But there was no time to think any longer. Marilen was waiting. The moment had come. He put his hands to his waist, unfastened the glittering belt, and let it fall. He heard Jasmine and Barda gasp.

Marilen pushed back her cloak. There was a flash of gleaming color. Then she was taking something from her own waist and handing it to Lief. Smiling with relief she moved quickly away to stand at a little distance.

The great jewels of the Belt of Deltora shone like stars under the morning sky. The exquisite links of steel gleamed warm in Lief's hands. He put the Belt on, felt its familiar weight, straightened his shoulders, and turned to face Barda and Jasmine.

They were staring, open-mouthed.

"The real Belt was safe in Del all the time!" Barda roared. "You were wearing a *copy*! All this time — and we did not know!" He scooped up the fallen belt and shook it in Lief's face. "*This* . . . this really *is* just a jewelled trifle!"

Lief nodded, shamefaced. "You have a right to be angry, both of you, but I beg you will understand," he muttered. "Doom and I made the copy in secret at the forge. We arranged our meetings using coded messages — just a simple code where each letter was replaced by the one following it in the alphabet and the numbers were treated likewise."

"So 'DOOM' would be 'EPPN,' " said Jasmine, remembering the note she had found.

Lief glanced at her curiously. "We used gems from the palace jewels that most nearly matched the real ones," he went on. "They have a little power of their own, as all great gems do, but compared to the talismans in the real Belt, they are worthless."

He smiled wryly. "Tirral felt no magic in the belt for very good reason. There was no magic in it!"

"You — you left the real Belt behind, to keep it safe," Jasmine stammered. "Your — your friend — wore it because — because she was the one you most trusted?"

"Because she was the one who *had* to wear it!" Lief answered. "In case anything happened to me." He beckoned to Marilen, who moved back to join them.

"Marilen is my distant cousin — my nearest relation on my father's side," Lief said, with a touch of pride. He laughed as Jasmine and Barda looked politely baffled. "Do you not see, you two?" he cried. "Marilen is my heir — the next in line to the Belt of Deltora."

"*What?*" Barda exploded.

"But — " Jasmine's voice caught in her throat.

She swallowed and tried again. "But I thought only the child of a king or queen could be the heir."

Lief nodded, unconsciously reaching for her hand. "The palace chief advisors encouraged that belief, because they were secret servants of the Shadow Lord," he said. "But when I thought about it, I knew it could not be true. It is far too dangerous for Deltora. My life was threatened from the moment I became king, and I had no child to wear the Belt after me, should I die."

It was such a relief to tell the story at last. The words, so long held back, tumbled from him in a stream. "*The Belt of Deltora* says simply that the Belt must be worn by Adin's true heir," he said. "It follows, then, that if a king or queen dies childless, the Belt will join with the next in line — a brother or sister, for example."

"But you have no brothers or . . . or sisters," said Jasmine, biting her lip as the last word brought back unpleasant memories.

Lief held her hand more tightly. "No. Or uncles and aunts, for that matter. It has been the royal habit to have one child only. By chance, Adin's heir had only one child, and this became the tradition — one the chief advisors insisted upon."

"It suited them very well, no doubt, to have the fate of Deltora hanging on one frail life in each generation," muttered Barda.

"Yes!" Lief said. "And they had done their work

so well that at first my attempts to find an heir seemed hopeless. But then — " He glanced at Marilen. "But then I remembered that Adin himself had several children."

"All of them married Torans," said Jasmine slowly. "Jinks told me that."

"Exactly," Lief said, wincing at the name of Jinks, as did Marilen, for a different reason. "So I knew that if I looked long and hard enough, I would surely find myself an heir in Tora, no matter how distant a relation he or she might be." He smiled slightly. " 'Blood is blood, no matter how thinly it is spread over the ages,' as someone said to us not long ago."

"So you searched the library books and parchments for clues," murmured Jasmine. "Family histories, records of marriages, children born . . . all those hours of work!"

"I had to secure Deltora's future before I could do anything else," Lief said. "And I had to do it in secret. Doom and my mother were the only ones I told. They knew how vital it was. They knew that Deltora's safety must never again depend on the life of just one person."

He smiled. "Marilen is a descendant of Adin's second son. When I found her, I knew I had my heir at last. It is true that when I have a child, that child will take her place as first in line — "

"That time cannot come soon enough for me!" Marilen broke in fervently. "When Lief told us in Tora that through my mother's family I was his heir, the news seemed more like a curse than a blessing."

Lief smiled at her fondly. "But still she agreed to leave her home, family, and friends and come to Del — "

"To wear the real Belt of Deltora if you went into danger, so that if something ill befell you, it would shine at once for her!" Jasmine burst out, finishing for him. "And all the time we thought — everyone thought . . ."

She pulled her hand from Lief's and put it to her burning face. Her head was spinning. So much that she had thought was not true. So many things she had seen one way, she now saw in another. Lief shutting himself away in the library. The parchment labelled *The Great Families of Tora*. The secret visits to the forge. The taking of the royal jewels. The visit to Tora itself . . .

"I know Lief wanted to tell you and Barda of me, Jasmine," Marilen said softly, seeing her distress. "But he had sworn to my father that only Sharn would know who I was, aside from Doom."

"The more people who knew Marilen was next in line, the more danger there was for her," Lief added. "If the Shadow Lord heard even a whisper . . ."

Jasmine swallowed and nodded. "Then why do you tell us now?" she managed to say.

Marilen smiled delightedly. "Because *now* all is well!" she exclaimed. "Lief had time only to trace the line of Adin's second child. But Adin and Zara, his wife, had *five* children in all. Zeean and my father examined the parchments Lief brought to Tora. They have discovered many more of Adin's descendants, not only in Tora, but in Del, too, and indeed all over the kingdom!"

She clasped her hands, her eyes sparkling. "Soon everyone will know that a threat to Lief is no longer a threat to the whole of Deltora. There will be no point in killing him — for that reason, at least."

"So I will no longer have to live in the palace, shut up like a prisoner!" exclaimed Lief with great satisfaction.

"And neither will I," said Marilen, equally happily. "If Lief should die childless, I will take his place. If I should die in my turn, there will be another to take *my* place — and another, and another, and another! The Belt will always find an heir, and Deltora is safe."

"What is all this talk of dying?" cried Barda clapping Lief on the shoulder and smiling broadly. "Though I confess I could strangle Lief myself when I think of the terrors I suffered, fearing for him and that lying belt!"

Marilen laughed. "I am so glad, so *glad*, that all this has ended in happiness," she said.

Jasmine nodded, still finding it difficult to think in different terms of Marilen. "This time must have been hard for you," she said, rather awkwardly.

"Indeed it has," Marilen said frankly. "I faced no

real danger compared to you, however. I had the Belt of Deltora, so I knew Lief lived, for it never shone for me. And the gems aided me. Once, the amethyst dimmed when my food was poisoned. I saw it, and knew something was amiss."

Her face broke into a smile. "Besides," she added, "if I had not come here, I would not have met Ranesh!"

She looked around to where Ranesh still stood alone on the stairs, forlornly looking after her. "I must go to him," she said. "I have much to explain. To him, and to poor Josef, too."

With another smile, she left them.

Lief raised his eyebrows. "So," he murmured. "Marilen and Ranesh." He glanced at Jasmine. He had sometimes had fears about Jasmine's feeling for Ranesh.

But Jasmine's smile as she met his eyes was very real. A great peace descended on Lief's heart.

Then Marilen turned around. "By the by, Lief," she called, "it seems that everyone believed I had come to Del to be your bride. Did you know?"

Lief's astounded expression was her answer. She laughed, and went on her way.

Lief swung round to Jasmine and Barda. "Had you heard this tale?" he demanded.

Barda remained expressionless, preserving wise silence. Jasmine's cheeks were burning again, but she shrugged. "Palace gossip," she said carelessly. "But you are far too young to marry. I always said so."

Lief was speechless.

Barda caught sight of Tira wandering towards the stairs, looking lost. He muttered something and strode off towards her.

"Of course," Jasmine went on, beginning to smile as she and Lief walked slowly after him. "Marilen would have been an ideal choice as a king's bride. Well read, beautiful, polite, elegant, at home in palaces . . ."

"When the time comes," Lief said, determinedly drowning her out, "I will follow Adin's example and marry for love." He glanced at her. "If the woman I love will have me, of course."

"She probably will," said Jasmine. "When the time comes." She slipped her hand into his.

A tumult of shouting and cheering began behind them. A great crowd was surging up the road from the city to join the crowd already thronging the lawn. The people on the stairs were laughing and beckoning. The bells were still ringing. Lief's heart swelled with joy.

And now, he thought. Now, at last, we can begin.